TRAIL OF VENGEANCE
THE CROCKETTS' WESTERN SAGA: 1

ROBERT VAUGHAN

WOLFPACK
PUBLISHING
— EST 2013 —

WOLFPACK PUBLISHING
— EST 2013 —

Published in the United States by Wolfpack Publishing, Las Vegas

Wolfpack Publishing
5130 S. Fort Apache Road, 215-380
Las Vegas, NV 89148

wolfpackpublishing.com

Paperback ISBN 978-1-64734-720-8
eBook ISBN 978-1-64734-719-2

TRAIL OF VENGEANCE

Chapter One

Wilson's Creek, Missouri – August 10th, 1861

There had been fierce fighting for the last two hours, and if Will or Gideon Crockett had to give an honest account of who was winning the battle, neither would be able to say. Will was a lieutenant and Gid was a sergeant in Captain Kirby's Company of General Sterling Price's Division, and so far they had seen nearly half of their company killed or so badly wounded as to be taken from the field.

During a pause in the fighting the men were eating some hardtack that had been fried in bacon grease. Will was paring a fresh peach that he had taken from a peach tree that had been picked clean over the last two days. He cut the peach in half, then held it out to Gid.

"Here you go, little brother," he said. Calling Gid his

"little" brother was left over from when the two were children. Then Gideon, who was the younger of the two, had been the smaller. Now Gid was taller and more muscular than his older brother.

"Lieutenant, I believe them Yankees is a' gettin' ready to come at us again," one of his men said.

"I believe you're right, Dooley," Will replied.

"They's goin' to be a whole bunch of 'em a' comin," Dooley suggested.

"That's true enough, but I want you to think about this. Those poor bastards are going to have to cross an open field to get to us. And where will we be?"

"I reckon we'll be a' waitin' for 'em behind this here stone fence."

"Which would you rather be? Coming across an open field, or waiting behind a stone fence?"

Dooley grinned. "Well, if you put it like that, I reckon I'd rather be right where I'm a sittin'."

Will nodded his head. "I thought you might see it like that."

"Hell, I say let the sons of bitches come at us," Gid said, joining the conversation. "I've got a few scores to settle."

Less than an hour later, two Yankee artillery pieces fired. That was merely the opening of a bombardment carried on by a score of Yankee cannons. Will and Gid were hunkered down behind the stone fence as the missiles whistled and whizzed overhead. The cannon balls were bursting within the ranks of the Confederate soldiers, who were waiting for the inevitable attack that would follow.

The cannonading continued for more than an hour, with enough of the shells falling onto the waiting Confederate soldiers that serious casualties were inflicted. Will learned of one of the casualties when the first sergeant came crawling down the line toward him.

"Lieutenant Crockett, Cap'n Kirby just got hisself kilt," the first sergeant said. "A cannon ball burst right on top of 'im. It looks like you're in command now."

"Are you sure he's dead?"

"Seein' as how I saw that cannon ball blow Cap'n Kirby into pieces, I'd say, yes sir, I'm damn sure."

Will's non-verbal response consisted only of a nod.

"What'll we do now, Lieutenant?" the first sergeant asked.

"We'll do just what Captain Kirby had in mind for us to do. We'll wait until they're right on us, then we'll kill as many as we can."

At that moment the Union artillery ceased fire, and the loud thunder that had been washing across the field, grew silent—so silent that Will could actually hear the sound of a woodpecker in the forest behind them, and the buzz of a swarm of flies around some congealed bacon grease.

Then he heard the long roll of drums in the Yankee ranks.

"Here they come!" someone shouted, though his warning wasn't necessary.

"The Yankees is attackin'!"

"They're fixin' to come at us!"

From his position behind the stone wall, Will could see the Yankee soldiers stretching out their line on the other side of the field.

As the commanding officer, Will stood up behind what was left of his company in order to exercise command and control over his men. It also had the effect of inspiring his men because while they could hide behind the stone wall, their commanding officer was exposing himself to enemy fire.

For the moment, all was quiet, save for the steady, rhythmic tat of the drums keeping the Yankee soldiers in line as they started their advance. They were still too far away to separate the individual soldiers from the mass of blue, but Will could see the flags fluttering in the breeze as the flag bearers took the lead position in front of each of the committed units.

Slowly, steadily, inexorably, the Yankee soldiers moved across the field.

"Steady, men, hold your fire, hold your position," Will ordered.

The drum beat cadence grew louder, and as the

advancing army moved closer, Will could hear the clank and rattle of their equipment, and the fall of their footsteps on the open ground.

"Stay in line men, stay in line!" a Yankee officer called as he marched in front with a raised saber. Will admired the courage it took for this young officer to be exposed the way he was.

To be honest, Will didn't think he had ever seen a more magnificent sight, nor a more foolish one. What officer in his right mind would expose his men in such a way?

Suddenly one of the advancing officers shouted out an order, and with that shout the advancing soldiers stopped their measured march and broke into a run, and now five thousand throats roared their defiance.

Confederate artillery opened fire on the attacking soldiers, and Will saw the awful effect of the grape and canister as it tore into the Yankee lines.

"Fire!" Will shouted, and not only his own men, but Confederate soldiers all up and down what would come to be called "Bloody Hill" began shooting.

For a moment Will was so engrossed in the battle that he forgot that he was standing in the open. Then he heard the angry buzz of Minie balls flying by him, and he moved quickly to the stone fence. That was when he saw the dashing young Yankee officer who was leading the charge, go down.

The deadly musket fire, to say nothing of the sustained grape and canister artillery fire, devastated the Yankee advance so that quickly, the five-thousand-man massed front was broken into smaller units. Several of the Yankee soldiers actually managed to cross the stone wall where they engaged in hand to hand combat with the Confederates, but by now, the Yankee ranks had been so decimated that they were overwhelmed. Those who could, retreated across the broad field leaving the dead and dying behind them.

Gradually, the constant bang and pop of gunfire died out. All that could be heard were the moans and cries of the wounded and the shouts coming from soldiers in both blue and gray, who were calling for assistance from hospital corpsman.

Will looked around for his brother and saw that Gid had come through the fray without being wounded. Will walked over to sit on the stone fence and look back across the field, which was now covered with a low-lying cloud of gun smoke. The smoke was so thick that he couldn't see the other side. What he did see, were the bodies of the dead, strewn across the field.

"What do you think, Will?" Gid asked. "Do you think General Price will want us to counter attack?"

"Not unless he wants to leave as many gray-clad bodies out there as there are blue, now," Will replied.

6

Chapter Two

Sergeant Gideon Crockett tossed a rock into the flowing stream that was Wilson Creek.

"Don't do that, there's some damn good crappie in that creek and you're scaring them away."

Gid chuckled. "Are you telling me that as my big brother, or are you ordering that because you're a lieutenant?"

"Both, I'm your older brother and I outrank you." The tone of Will's response was teasing, not challenging.

"But you're right; there really are some good crappie in this stream. Do you remember the first time Pa brought us here?" Gid asked.

"I sure do," Will said. "We caught a mess of 'em and Pa fried 'em up for our supper that night."

Gid walked away from the edge of the creek. "We whipped the Yankees pretty good today. You think they'll try us again tomorrow?"

"I heard some of the higher ranking officers talking. I think General Price aims to attack the Yankees head on," Will replied.

At first light, even as General Price's troops were preparing to attack, the Union surprised the Confederates by launching their own attack.

"Holy shit! The Yankees is a' comin'!" a man shouted.

Will needed no announcement; he could see the Union troops coming across the field led by General Lyon himself. The Yankee force soon overran the Confederate camps and took the high ground at the crest of a ridge.

"Lieutenant Crockett, what'll we do?" one of his men called out to him.

"The Yankees have the high ground, so all we can do now is throw as much lead at them as we can," Will answered.

The sound of rifle fire was soon augmented with the deep throated thump of heavy artillery fire.

"Ours, or theirs?" Gid called.

"Ours!" Will said happily. "It must be the Pulaski Arkansas Battery! That'll stop the Yankee advance!"

"Lieutenant Crockett, sir, General Price's compliments," a messenger said, running up to report to him. "He intends to advance to the south slope of Bloody Hill!"

"Very good, Corporal, thank you," Will replied.

"We'll move out."

Once the Confederate units, including Will's company, took position on Bloody Hill, they were able to halt the Yankee advance. The air was still alive with Minie balls and bursting cannon shells, but for the moment, the Yankee approach had been checked.

"I'll be damn if those sons of bitches aren't getting ready to come again," Gid said.

"Hold your fire men; hold your fire until they are almost right on us. I'll give the word," Will ordered.

Across the field the Yankees, now reorganized, mounted a counter attack.

"That looks like a general leadin' them," Gid said, squinting his eyes.

"It is. It's General Lyons," Will said.

"You have to give the son of a bitch credit for courage," Gid said begrudgingly.

Will and the others watched the Yankees assault until they were within a hundred yards.

"Now!" Will called and his men opened fire with a devastating volley. The Yankee charge was stopped

Colonel McCulloch led a Confederate counter attack, rallying several units, including Will's company. Shortly after they gained their objective, a major from General Price's staff came up.

"Lieutenant Crockett, where's Captain Kirby?" the

major asked.

"Captain Kirby was killed yesterday, sir," Will replied.

You're in command, then?"

"Yes, sir."

"All right, Lieutenant, close your company with Captain Quantrill and when ordered to do so, resume the advance."

"Yes, sir," Will replied.

Will brought his company up in line with Quantrill's. The two men placed themselves in front of the long line of skirmishers then, drawing their sabers and holding them up, shouted the order, "Advance!"

As the two companies moved toward the hill occupied by the Yankees, Will couldn't help but think of his earlier observation that, "it's easier to defend than attack." But here he was, leading his own company in this attack.

Yankee bullets whizzed by but he, with Quantrill beside him, continued the advance.

Yankee artillery fired, the thunder of the big guns easily heard even in the din of rifle fire. The shells burst within the body of troops behind him, and Will knew his company was taking heavy casualties, but he continued forward.

A Yankee bullet hit his raised saber cutting it in two and knocking it from his hand. Without pause, Will picked up the stub of the saber and again, raised it over his head.

Though Will and Quantrill's companies were in the vanguard of the attack, by now the entire Confederate army had gone from defense to offense as they surged across the field toward the Yankees.

Will and Quantrill's companies closed with the enemy, and the Yankees who were manning the cannons abandoned their pieces and fled to the rear.

The surging Confederate troops gave an exultant shout of victory as the Yankees retreated.

With the combined Confederate units moving up the hill, the Yankee forces led by Colonel Sigel fled the field, leaving behind the four abandoned cannons. This left Generals Lyon and Sweeny, and Colonel Sturgis' troops exposed to the swarm of Confederate attackers and the momentum of the battle shifted in the South's favor.

"Stand fast, men, stand fast!" Will heard General Lyon yell in an attempt to rally his troops.

Then Will saw something that so disheartened the Yankee troops that the tide of battle was changed. General Lyon was struck in the heart and killed. General Sweeny was hit, as well. With their commanding general dead, the second general down, and supplies low, Union morale was worsening. Finally Colonel Sturgis, who had taken command of the Yankee troops retreated rather than risk a fourth Confederate attack.

After the battle, with the Yankees gone and the Confederates now occupying the field, General Price sent for both William Crockett and William Clark Quantrill.

"You have any idea what this is about?" Will asked.

"No, I don't know," Quantrill replied.

When the two men reported to their Commander, General Price called his staff to attention, and then read from a document.

"Captain William Quantrill and Lieutenant William Crockett are, by these presence, cited for bravery and performance of duty in that they did expose themselves to intense enemy fire providing an inspiration to the men in their commands.

"Lieutenant Crockett is hereby promoted to Captain and given permanent command of his company.

By order of General Sterling Price, Commanding.

With Will's promotion to Captain, he was given the opportunity to select his own lieutenant and he chose his brother, Gideon.

December, 1861

General Price's army was in bivouac near Springfield, Missouri, when Frank McCain came over to visit with Will and Gid. Because the McCain family farm was adjacent to the Crockett farm, Frank had grown up with Will and Gid, and the three men were great, personal friends.

"I just came by to let you boys know that I'm getting out of here," Frank said.

"Getting out of here? What do you mean? Are you deserting?" Will asked.

"No, I'm not deserting, I'm going with Quantrill."

"I don't understand, you're already with Quantrill."

Frank smiled. "Quantrill is starting his own regiment."

"They're giving Quantrill a regiment? How can that be? There are several other officers who are senior to him."

"Oh, nobody is giving him a regiment; he's starting his own," Frank said.

"His own regiment? For crying out loud, Frank, you aren't making any sense. What are you talking about?"

At that moment Captain Quantrill approached the three men. "Did you tell them my plan, Frank?" Quantrill asked.

"Yes, sir, I did."

"What do you think, Captain Crockett?" Quantrill asked. "I'm leaving Price's Division. Do you and your brother want to come with me? You're both good fighters, I've seen you in action."

"What do you mean you're leaving?" Will asked. "Sterling Price is the best general we have in the West—you know that yourself."

"Didn't Frank tell you? I'm going to start my own

regiment," Quantrill said. "I won't be a part of Price's Division, or Van Dorn's, or any other general. I'll be completely independent, serving the Confederate cause, but in my own way."

"You're talking about starting an outfit of irregulars, aren't you?"

Quantrill raised his eyebrows. "You could say that, I guess."

"Where will you get your soldiers?"

"I don't expect I'll have too much trouble recruiting men who really want to fight. Your friend here has already joined. I'd like to have you two come with us."

"I appreciate the invitation, Captain Quantrill, but I think we'll stay where we are," Will said.

"Colonel."

"I beg your pardon."

"If I'm going to start my own regiment, I intend to be a colonel."

"You can't just appoint yourself a colonel," Gid said.

"Why not? Rich men all over the South have raised money to arm and equip a regiment and are given the rank of colonel to lead the regiment. I'll be starting my own regiment, so how is this any different?"

Will laughed. "If you put it that way, I don't know that there would be any difference."

"I'm glad you see it that way," Quantrill said. "And I

want you to know that even if you don't join me now, you can join me anytime you want. The invitation is always open to you two."

"We'll keep that in mind," Will said.

Pea Ridge, Arkansas – March 1862

By spring of 1862, Union forces had pushed General Sterling Price out of Missouri and into Arkansas. There, Price and his command were put under the command of Major General Earl Van Dorn.

"General Price is pissed because he isn't in overall command," Will said. "So we can damn well count on him getting us right in the thick of things as soon as he can."

On the night of March 6th, Van Dorn's army with Sterling Price's Division leading, began the long march to Cross Timber Hollow. General Price sent for Will Crockett.

"Captain Crockett, General Van Dorn has given my division the honor of leading us into battle," General Price said. "I have chosen your company to be the vanguard not only in the attack, but you will also be the first element of our long road march."

"Thank you, General. I am honored to have been chosen," Will replied.

When Will returned to his command Gid was the first

one to meet him.

"What did the general have to say?"

"We've got a long night walk in front of us," Will replied.

Once they got underway they were significantly slowed by the necessity of having to clear obstructions. Van Dorn had planned for both his divisions to reach Cross Timber Hollow in the middle of the night, but by dawn, only the head of Price's division, including Will's company, had made it that far. Because of the delay, Van Dorn instructed McCulloch's division to take the Ford Road from Twelve Corner Church and meet Price at Elkhorn.

That morning an advanced scout reported to Will.

"Cap'n, there's Yankee patrols out, 'n I think they done seen us."

"All right," Will said, "we've set out to attack them, but it looks like we may wind up on the defense."

Will's observation proved to be true when several cavalry units launched the attack.

"How many are there, Captain?" McCulloch asked.

"General, I know only the troops I have encountered," Will replied. "My guess would be at least fifteen hundred in front of me."

"I need to be sure," McCulloch replied. McCulloch rode forward into the belt of timber to personally reconnoiter the Federal positions, and coming into range of the skirmishers was shot through the heart. McIntosh was quickly notified that he was in command, but his staff, fearing that the death of their popular leader would dishearten his soldiers, made the unwise decision not to share the bad news with many of the subordinate officers. Without consulting anyone else, McIntosh impulsively led his former regiment, the dismounted 2nd Arkansas Mounted Rifles Regiment, into the attack. As the unit reached the southern edge of the belt of timber, it was met with a massed volley from Yankee forces, and like McCulloch before him, McIntosh was killed.

At this point, Colonel Elkanah Greer would normally have taken command but he had not been told that both McCulloch and McIntosh had been killed. In the meantime, Brigadier General Albert Pike who, although outside the normal chain of command of McCulloch's division, was the highest ranking officer, so he assumed command. His first act was to order a retreat.

"Retreat?" Will said. "Sergeant, are you sure General Pike has ordered a retreat?"

"Yes, sir, that's what he said."

"Gid," Will called. "Hold the company here, there has to be some mistake. I'm going to talk to General Pike myself."

Following the messenger sergeant's directions, Will

found General Pike, not in front of his troops where the other generals were usually found, but behind the lines, hunkered down behind a hill.

"General, is it true you have ordered a retreat?" Will asked.

"I have. It is my intention to withdraw to Twelve Corners Church."

"But why, General? We have the Yankees outnumbered, and we have field advantage over them."

"Captain, I'll not have you question my orders," General Pike said. "I have ordered a withdrawal and I expect my orders to be followed."

The retreat took place in total confusion with at least one regiment ordered to discard its arms and bury them for later recovery. Pike's retreat turned into a rout that spread throughout the entire Confederate army. Several regiments and even some divisions who were prevailing on the battlefield, lost their tactical advantage so that they, too, were forced to retreat.

The Confederates, in spite of their superior numbers, lost the battle of Pea Ridge.

Chapter Three

St. Leger, Missouri – April, 1862

It had been over a year since Will and Gid had seen their parents, and with General Price's Division bivouacked outside of Springfield, the two brothers took a leave of absence to go home. Home was the Crockett Farm just north of St. Leger, and they reached the town in mid-afternoon.

"Say, Will, before we go out to the farm, what do you say we stop at the saloon and wash some of the trail dust out of our throats," Gid suggested.

Will laughed. "Why, little brother, are you suggesting that you don't think Ma will greet us with a couple of beers?"

"Are you kidding? What is it she calls it? The devil's brew?"

"You're right, if we're going to have a drink we'd better

have it now, before we go out to see the folks."

They tied their horses off in front of an establishment called Nippy Jones Tavern, and were greeted by Nippy Jones himself when they stepped inside.

"Well, I didn't know when I would see you boys again," Jones said as he drew a mug of beer for each of them. "It's been what? A year?"

"A little longer," Will answered.

"Who else is around?" Gid asked.

"Frank McCain was in yesterday. Loomis Sutton and Andy Gutherie were here last week. And the Hallman brothers have been in a few times." Nippy Jones was quiet for a moment. "They're wearing the blue," he added.

"Yes, I heard that they were."

"We've got a good mix here," Nippy added. "About as many boys in blue as we have in gray."

"Yes, I expect most of Missouri is like that," Will said. "Has it ever caused any trouble?"

"I can't say that it has. There's been times when I've had blue and gray in here at the same time, but they was friends before the war 'n turns out that they're still friends even if they's on different sides."

"Good," Will said, "I'm glad to hear that."

"One more before we go," Gid said, pushing his, now-empty mug toward Nippy.

"Yeah, me too," Will said.

Crockett Farm

When Drury Crockett reached the end of the field he hauled back on the reins.

"Whoa, there, Rhoda," he called out to his mule. "Take a breather there old girl."

Rhoda, as if understanding, responded with a whickering sound.

Drury draped the reins over his shoulders and wiped the sweat from his face. He smiled as he saw Amanda coming toward him. She was carrying a jug.

"I made you some sweet tea."

"Why are you being so nice to me? Are you trying to get me to marry you or something?" Drury asked as he reached for the jug.

Amanda laughed. "You old fool, we've been married for thirty-two years."

"Is that what that business in the church was all about?" Drury lifted the jug to his lips and began drinking.

"That's what it was all about."

Drury drank almost half the tea before he lowered the jug. "Well, I'll tell you the truth, if we weren't already hitched, I'd marry ya today." A broad smile crossed his face.

"Well now, Mr. Crockett, just what makes you think

I'd marry you?"

"So Will and Gid would have a papa?"

"They'd probably appreciate that."

"Speaking of Will and Gid, they said they'd be here sometime today. If they was here now, I'd sure put them to work plowin' this dirt."

"You would not!" Amanda said. "Do you think after all the fighting they've been in they'd want to start workin' in the field first thing after they get home?"

"Given what those boys have been through, I expect they might prefer plowing a field over gettin' shot at."

"If you put it that way, I guess you're right. I hope they're hungry whenever they get here, 'cause I've made a big pot of chicken 'n dumplin's," Amanda said.

"What do you mean, you hope they're hungry? This is Will and Gid we're talking about."

Amanda chuckled. "You've got that right. Oh, Look! Riders are comin'. It must be them!" She started to run toward the house.

"It's about time they got here."

"Drury?" Amanda said suddenly. There was a tightness in her voice. "It's not them."

Drury turned to look in the direction she was pointing and saw a group of riders approaching.

Drury and Amanda watched as the riders came toward them. They were wearing blue.

"Is this the Crockett farm?" the leader of the group asked. He was a big man, and he had a scar on his face that disfigured his left eye.

"It is," Drury replied.

"I am Captain Otto Hoffman. We are looking for William and Gideon Crockett. I believe they are your sons, and I've been told that they would be here."

"They are our sons, but they aren't here," Drury replied.

"Where are they?" Hoffman asked.

"Right now they're with General Price." Drury smiled. "So if you want 'em, you can go get 'em."

A cruel smile spread across Hoffman's lips. "That's all right, I don't need them, as long as I have you two."

"What do you mean?" Amanda asked, frightened by the words.

"Grab her, boys," Hoffman said. "We'll have a little fun with her."

"The hell you will!" Drury shouted angrily, and lifting the jug from which he had been drinking, as his only weapon, he started toward Hoffman. At least three of Hoffman's men shot Drury, and he went down, dead before he hit the ground.

"Drury!" Amanda shouted in horror, starting toward the crumpled body of her husband.

Hoffman nodded, and two of the men grabbed Amanda.

"Now," Hoffman said, starting toward the distraught woman. He undid the belt that was holding up his pants. "I'm first, then the rest of you boys can decide among yourselves who gets her next."

"Hey, Will, do you think maybe Ma might have cooked up a pot of chicken 'n dumplin's for us?" Gid asked as the two rode along the road that led to the Crockett farm.

"Well, I don't know. Do you think tomorrow the sun will rise in the East?"

Gid laughed. "Yeah, I think she'll have 'em when we get there."

A little while later Will pointed ahead. "Gid, look at that smoke."

"My God, it looks like it's comin' from home!"

The brothers broke into a gallop, racing toward the smoke. When they arrived they saw that the house and the barn were burning, both buildings entirely invested with flames. Black smoke roiled into the sky.

"Where's Ma and Pa?" Gid asked as the two men looked in vain for their parents.

"There's Rhoda," Gid said. "What's she doin' standing out in the field all by herself?"

"My God, Gid, she's not by herself," Will said, pointing to two shapes on the ground.

Again, Will and Gid urged their horses into a gallop.

Even before they got to the middle of the field, they recognized the shapes on the ground. Their mother was naked, and leaping down from the saddles the two men hurried to their parents.

There were bullet holes in their father, and their mother had bruises all over her body and a bullet wound in her chest.

"Will! Ma's still alive!"

The two knelt beside their mother.

"Ma!" Will said, fighting the lump in his throat.

Amanda, seeing her son, smiled. "I prayed to stay alive until I could see the two of you one more time. My boys." She put her hand on first Will's cheek, then Gid's.

"I'm going to get the wagon so we can get you to the doctor," Gid said.

"No," Amanda answered. "Not now."

"Just to get the wagon," Gid said.

"No, please, God let me live to see you one more time. I know I'll die before you get the wagon. I want you to spend the rest of my time with me."

"Ma, who did this?" Will asked as he held her hand in his.

Amanda took a couple of gasping breaths. "Hoffman. He said his name was Otto Hoffman."

"Isn't he the leader of that bunch of redlegs?" Gid asked.

"That's him—the dirty rotten bastard."

"Move me over beside Drury," Amanda said. "I want

to be with him when ..." again, she had to gasp for breath.

"Don't talk, Ma, we'll move you to him."

Working together, the two men moved their mother as gently as possible to lay her beside their father's bullet-riddled body. Will placed Drury's hand in hers.

"Yes," Amanda said. "Yes, my sweet darling, I know you're waiting. I'll be there with you."

She took her last breath.

Garden of Memories Cemetery, St Leger

Drury and Amanda Crockett were well respected in the little town of St. Leger, and nearly the entire community had turned out for the funeral. There had been too many to fit into the church, but they came to the cemetery for the graveside rites. Father Pyron of St. Paul's Episcopal Church gave the committal prayer.

"Believing in the Resurrection to eternal life through our Lord Jesus Christ, we now entrust Drury and Amanda to the care of Almighty God and we ask Our Father to open the doors to his mansion and lead Drury and Amanda to the room made ready just for them. As we now commit their bodies to the ground, earth to earth, ashes to ashes, dust to dust, we commend their spirits to their new home. Rest eternal grant them and let light perpetual shine upon them."

Will and Gid remained standing at the grave sites after the service was concluded and the others had left, or were leaving.

"I know who done this."

Looking toward the sound of a familiar voice, the two brothers saw Frank McCain standing just behind them.

"How do you know?" Will asked, not suggesting that their mother had said a name.

"Because he's done this same thing half a dozen times before," Frank said. "His name's Otto Hoffman 'n he likes to kill people, then burn up their houses 'n barns 'n such. We been after 'im."

"We?"

"Quantrill."

"Oh, yes, Quantrill's irregulars. You're still with him?"

"Yes, and remember, he tried to recruit you two."

"You aren't trying that again are you? To recruit us for Quantrill?"

"Let me ask you boys something," Frank said. "Would you like to see Hoffman dead?"

"I not only want to see him dead, I want to personally kill the son of a bitch," Will said.

"Do you think General Sterling Price is going to go after Hoffman?"

"Probably not."

Frank smiled. "Quantrill will."

Chapter Four

July 8th, 1863 – Lee's Summit, Missouri

Will and Gid had been with Quantrill for well over a year. They were camped in one of their regular campsites that they called the bull pen. This made a good hideout for the raiders because it was situated in the dense woods about a mile from Cedar Creek. There were two ways of approaching the Bull Pen: one through the creek bottom and the other through the woods south of a farm owned by a Confederate sympathizer.

One day Will, Gid, and about twenty other men started south to Big Creek, near the town of Lee's Summit.

Will, who had retained his captaincy when he joined Quantrill, was in command. He had sent a point rider out, and that rider now came galloping back.

"What is it, Barnhill?" Will asked.

"Cap'n, there's a bunch of Jayhawkers ahead," Barnhill said.

"Hoffman?"

"No, sir, I didn't see him."

"How many are there?"

"Thirty at least, maybe forty," Barnhill answered.

"Cap'n, are we goin' to try 'n ride around 'em without bein' seen, none?

Tom Hayes asked.

Will smiled and shook his head. "No, we're goin' to attack 'em."

"But aren't we a little outnumbered?" Hayes asked.

"I wouldn't worry about that," Will said. "Hell, most Yankees can't count anyway."

Will's response brought a chuckle from the others and steeled them for the opportunity to fight.

Will and his raiders charged the Yankees before they realized they had been spotted. Instead of standing to fight, the Jayhawkers scattered and Will and his men gave chase. By the end of the fight, seven of the Jayhawkers had been killed. Had Will known about it he would have taken particular pleasure in the operation, because two of the seven killed had been with Hoffman on the day the Crockett farm was raided.

August 13, 1863 - Longhorn Tavern, Kansas City, Missouri

The third floor had been converted into a woman's prison. The women in the prison were incarcerated because they were related in one way or another to members of Quantrill's Raiders.

Josephine Anderson was 18 years old, her sisters Mary and Mattie were 16 and 13. All three were the sisters of Bloody Bill Anderson. Susan and Matilda Mundy, both 21, had a brother serving with General Price. One of the women had purchased a large amount of cloth for the supposed purpose of making guerrilla shirts. When the Union troopers discovered the cloth and the shirts in her home, she too was arrested. The Crawford sisters, Susan Crawford Vandever and Armenia Crawford Selvey had husbands who served under General Joseph O. Shelby. It was determined that the sisters had purchased too much medicine for their families personal use, so they were accused of giving aid and comfort to the enemy and they were arrested.

Another of the women prisoners was Charity McCorkle Kerr. Charity's husband, Nathan Kerr, and her two brothers, John and Jabez McCorkle, all rode with Quantrill.

The women had complained about overcrowding and unsafe conditions. To make extra space available, it was said that the Union soldiers removed some support beams of the brick structure. Three beams had been cut away from the center beam even though the remaining building supports had already sunk some two or three feet.

The plastering had been falling all day and the women were in a panic. Then the building cracked and crumbled to the ground with seventeen women, one boy and one guard inside. All were injured, and in some cases the injuries proved to be fatal.

September 20, 1863 – Lawrence, Kansas

The demand for revenge for the killing of their women was very high, so on the morning of September 20th, Quantrill gave the orders to break camp and proceed to Lawrence, Kansas. The reason he had chosen that target was because there was a company of Union soldiers stationed in the town and Quantrill proposed to go after them. There would be more Union soldiers than raiders, but Quantrill realized that he would have the advantage of surprise.

After an all-night ride, they reached the town of Lawrence just at daylight.

"Gentlemen," Quantrill said. "This is the home of Jim Lane and Otto Hoffman. Remember that in hunting us they gave no quarter, nor will we. There are Yankee soldiers here. Shoot everyone you see, but in no way harm a woman or a child."

31

"Will, do you think Otto Hoffman is here?" Gid asked.

"I hope he is," Will replied. "I certainly hope he is."

Quantrill gave the order to attack and the raiders galloped down the street, shooting soldiers in uniform, and setting a dozen or more fires. They found Hoffman's house and Will, Gid, and four others rushed inside.

Hoffman wasn't there, but they found his saber which was kept in a gold plated scabbard.

"Hey, Cap'n, come in here 'n look at this!" one of the men called.

Responding to the summons, Will went into the parlor where he saw three beautiful grand pianos. Two of the pianos had belonged to Southern sympathizers who lived in the county where the Crockett farm had been.

"Look here at all this silverware," Will said pointing to a large pile of cutlery.

"He is one thieving son of a bitch," Gid said.

As they searched through the house, they were aware of constant gunfire coming from outside.

"Come on, boys," Will said. "Sounds like the Yankees are putting up a fight."

When the raiders left two hours later the town was in ashes, and 175 Jayhawkers were dead. Very much to Will's disappointment, Otto Hoffman was nowhere to be found.

Although Quantrill had given orders against shooting women or children, many got caught in the crossfire, and the death of those innocents would forever color public opinion of the raid on Lawrence, Kansas.

October, 1863 – Blue Creek Crossing, Missouri

The Tenth Kansas had come to the little town of Blue Creek Crossing as payback for the Lawrence raid. They had camped out the night before and now, as the first light of the morning illuminated the town before them, they got into position for their attack.

"Remember," Hoffman said. "Shoot any male you see, no matter how old."

"Kids too?" one of his men asked.

"Why not? They'll just grow up to be Rebels," Hoffman said.

"General, some Missourians are Union."

"Most of 'em here are Rebels, so if we kill 'em all, we're certain to get the Rebels."

As Hoffman and his Jayhawkers rode into town they saw an old, gray-haired man and a young boy. This was Marvin Collins and his seven year old grandson, Nicky. They were leading a cow from the barn, and they looked up in curiosity.

"Hey, old man," Hoffman called. "Are there any more men in your house?"

"No, my son is away."

"Union, or Secesh?"

"He's ..." the man started to say but his response was interrupted by Hoffman shooting him between the eyes.

"Grandpa!" the boy shouted.

Hoffman shot him down as well.

"Now we won't know if he was Union or a Reb," one of the men said.

"It don't matter none, I told you to shoot every male you see," Hoffman said. "Actually, make that everyone you see, man or woman."

When neighbors, alerted by the gunshot, came out to see what was going on, their curiosity got them killed.

After the initial few shootings, Hoffman led his men down through the middle of town and they began shooting, targeting man and boy, woman and girl. When they rode out of town half an hour later, 211 people lay dead behind them, and every business building in town was burning.

Aubrey, Kansas

Three weeks after the Blue Creek Crossing raid, Quantrill and his men were alongside the road that led into Aubrey.

"Are you sure Hoffman is coming this way, Colonel?" Will asked.

"That's our information," Quantrill replied.

"I suppose you want Hoffman for yourself," Frank

James said as the men got into position for the ambush.

"I want him killed by either me or by my brother."

Frank laughed. "Yeah, that's the way it is with Jesse and me."

"Here they come, Colonel!" someone called.

"Get in position," Quantrill ordered.

"It looks like they've got us outnumbered," McCain said.

"It doesn't matter how many there are," Quantrill said. "We have the advantage of position and surprise."

"I don't feel good about this, Will," Gid said in a quiet voice. "I mean, it feels to me like we're just shootin' 'em down without any warning."

"This is war, Gid. Besides how much warning did they give Ma and Pa?"

"Yeah," Gid agreed. "How much warning did they give Ma and Pa?"

The ambush was quick and effective, and in less than half an hour all ten Jayhawkers lay dead in the road.

"Damn," Will said in frustration after he examined all the bodies. "Neither Hoffman nor Felix Martin was with them." Felix Martin, they had learned, was second in command of Hoffman's raiders, and he had been with Hoffman on the day their parents had been killed.

"We'll find the bastards someday," Gid said, "and when we do find them, we'll kill them."

April 20th, 1865

After three years of riding with Quantrill, including the infamous raid on Lawrence, Kansas, the raiders learned that a couple of weeks earlier, on the 9th of April, in Appomattox, Virginia, Robert E Lee had surrendered his army to Ulysses S. Grant.

"You mean the war's over?" Josh McCorkle, one of the raiders asked.

"It may be over for some people," Quantrill replied. "But it's not over for me, and it's not over for those of you who are willing to continue the fight with me."

"Where are you a' goin', Colonel?" one of the raiders asked.

"I'm going to Kentucky."

"We'll not be going to Kentucky," Will said.

"Why not?" Quantrill asked. "You and your brother are two of my best men."

"Hoffman and Martin aren't in Kentucky, they're in Kansas," Will said. "We've chased them for three years and haven't been able to get them."

"Hoffman and Martin aren't important," Quantrill replied, "at least, not in the broader scheme of things. It's time we took our battle to some of the regular Yankee army units."

"They are important to my brother and me," Will said.

Will and Gid weren't the only ones to leave Quantrill. Frank and Jesse James left as well, vowing to make the Yankees pay in cash.

Quantrill's Raiders ceased to exist as a premier fighting unit. Most of the men who had been with him had had enough war and decided to go home. A few, like the James brothers, took to the outlaw trail, and some went to Kentucky with Quantrill.

Frank McCain told Will and Gid that he was going to Texas.

"You should come with me," he said.

"Why Texas?"

"Why not? There's nothin' left for us up here. I figure on puttin' the war behind me 'n startin' all over again."

"Maybe someday we'll come there and look around," Will said. "But I don't plan to go anywhere until we've dealt with Hoffman and Martin."

June 15th, 1865

"Quantrill's dead," Hoffman announced with a broad smile.

"How do you know he's dead?" Felix Martin asked.

"It come in by telegram," Hoffman said. "He was kilt in Kentucky."

"Ha! Then there ain't no more Quantrill."

Conway Farm, Plain Grove, Missouri

When Hoffman, Martin, and eight of the men who were riding with him rode up to the house, Jerome Conway and his two sons, Moe and Dewey, stepped out to meet them.

"Have you been riding long?" Jerome asked. "If so, feel free to water your horses." He pointed to the watering trough. "It's full."

Conway didn't really feel all that neighborly at the moment because there was something about these men that frightened him, but he tried to hide that fear with his friendly offer.

"You're Captain Conway?" Hoffman asked.

"I was," Conway replied. "But the war's over and now I'm just plain old Farmer Conway." He forced a smile.

"We're lookin' for Frank and Jesse James and Will and Gid Crockett. We hear you're friends of theirs."

"I've never heard of 'em," Conway said.

Hoffman's smile could only be described as evil. "That's too bad."

Conway had lied to Hoffman. He did know Will and Gid and in fact they had been invited for dinner at the Conway farm that very evening, but when they arrive at the Conway farm two hours later, they found Mrs.

Conway and her daughter Julie, standing on a rock. The women had their ankles tied together, and their wrists tied behind them. They each had a noose around their neck, and the noose was tied to a tree limb overhead. If either of them slipped or fell off the rock, they would be stepping into eternity.

From another limb, hanging so that the women could clearly see them, were the bodies of Jason Conway and his two sons, one of whom was only fifteen. The men had been hanged but the two women had remained tied on the rock, poised one half-step from death.

As soon as Will and Gid cut the women down, they collapsed from exhaustion, and it wasn't until after the men had been buried that they were recovered enough to tell what had happened.

"It was some Kansas raiders," Mrs. Conway said.

"Do you know who?" Will asked.

"The leader of the group said his name was Hoffman," Mrs. Conway said. "I don't have any idea who any of the others were."

"I heard one of 'em's name called out," the girl answered. "It was Felix Martin, or somethin' like that."

"Do you have any idea where they might have gone from here?"

Mrs. Conway shook her head. "We couldn't see 'em when they rode off, 'cause they was behind us."

Chapter Five

Beria, Kansas – May 9th, 1866

The war had been over for more than a year but Will and Gid's search for Otto Hoffman and Felix Martin continued. They had searched all through Western Missouri and Eastern Kansas without success. Now they were riding into the small town of Berea, brought here by a tip. The fact that the tip had come from a man who had once ridden with Hoffman gave Will the hope that, this time he would be successful.

"You know, big brother, we've never actually seen Otto Hoffman," Gid said. "The truth is he could walk right by us on the street, and we wouldn't even recognize the son of a bitch."

"I'll recognize him," Will said.

"How would you recognize him? From the descriptions? Good luck with that." Gid prodded his brother.

"I'll recognize him," Will said determinedly.

Will was able to put his theory to the test two days later when a man walked into the Frog City Saloon who fit the description Will had of Hoffman. The man was big, fully as large as Gid, with a full beard and long matted hair that was hanging from beneath a dirty, black hat. The telling feature, however, was the scar that cut down through his left eye.

There were three others with him, and the four men stepped up to the bar to order whiskey.

"Will?" Gid said.

"Yeah, it's him," Will replied.

"What are we going to do?"

"We've been chasing this son of a bitch for four years now, 'n I don't plan to let him get away."

"I wonder if one of them is Martin."

"We'll soon find out," Will replied.

"All right, call it."

"When it starts, you take the two on the left. I'll take Hoffman and the other one."

"Sounds like a good plan to me." Gid loosened the pistol in his holster.

"Otto Hoffman?" Will called out. The challenge in his voice was recognized by everyone in the saloon and all conversation stopped.

"What makes you think I'm Hoffman?"

"Because I was told to look for the ugliest son of a bitch I had ever seen, and that would be you."

"What do you want with me?" Hoffman asked.

"You remember visiting St. Leger, Missouri?" Will asked.

"I visited a lot of towns in Missouri during the war."

"You burned a farm there."

"I burned lots of farms."

"Yeah, well when you burned this farm, you also killed the innocent people you found there."

"There warn't no one in Missouri that was innocent during the war."

"That's where you're wrong. Drury and Amanda Crockett were innocent," Will said.

"So, you must be the Crocketts," Hoffman said. "I heard you boys were looking for me."

"I'm Will Crockett, this is my brother, Gid. I suppose now you can see why we are a might upset with you for killing them. They were our parents."

Hoffman turned to face him and as he did, the other three men turned as well, then they spread out, putting some distance between themselves thus presenting a more difficult target.

"Will, the odds don't look all that good," Gid said.

An evil smile appeared on Hoffman's face. "You don't like the odds, huh? Let me introduce you to my three friends. This here'n is Matthew, don't know if that's his first name or last name, he ain't never told me, 'n I'm not inclined to try 'n find out. The next one over says his name is Carter, 'n the feller standin' out there a ways," he added, pointing to the man who had positioned himself the farthest out, "is either Smith or Jones, I can't never keep his name straight 'n neither can he."

"So, Felix Martin isn't here."

"I ain't seen Martin around in a while," Hoffman said.

"Too bad he isn't here, that would make the odds a little better," Gid said. "There's only four of you, it seems almost a shame, us taking advantage of you like that."

At Gid's words the expression on Hoffman's face changed from smug confidence, to questioning anxiety.

"Now!" Hoffman shouted and he and the three men with him went for their guns.

Will and Gid made no attempt to go for their guns until after Hoffman and the other three started their draw. All four had actually cleared leather, and Hoffman, sure that he had won, was wearing a triumphant smile. The smile turned to shock when he saw guns appear as if by magic, in the hands of the two Crockett brothers.

The eight shots that were fired in the confrontation were so close together that it sounded like one sustained roar. Only Hoffman, Carter, and Matthew actually got a shot off. Smith/Jones died before he was able to bring his gun up to bear. None of the three shots fired by Hoffman, Matthew, and Carter found their mark. All four shots fired by Will and Gid hit their targets, resulting in a single fatal bullet wound in each of the four men.

"Son of a bitch! I ain't never seen nothin' like that!" one of the saloon patrons said in awe.

"I didn't think there was nobody faster 'n Matthew," another said.

While the saloon patrons gathered around the three bodies, the bartender came over to talk, quietly with Will and Gid.

"I think you two boys had best slip out the back door while you can," the bartender said.

"No need for that," Will said. "I think everyone in here saw that they drew first."

"That don't matter none," the bartender said. "You see, the way things is, this bein' Kansas 'n you two boys bein' from Missouri, it'd be best if you was to leave now."

"What does it matter that we're from Missouri? The war's over."

"Yeah, well, there's some folks around here that don't feel that way. You can mark my words that within two days them four boys you two fellers just kilt will be heroes 'n if you two is still around, you'll be hanged."

"I think we should pay attention to what he's saying, Will."

"Tell me, why are you willing to help us?"

The bartender smiled. "I'm from Missouri too, 'n from what I've heard about Hoffman, the son of a bitch needed killin'. Slip on out the back door now, before the sheriff gets here.

"We found Hoffman and took care of him, so where do we go now?" Gid asked as the two men rode out of town.

"Well, we could continue looking for Martin, or we could go back to the farm," Will said.

"I don't know," Gid replied.

"What do you mean, you don't know?"

"Will, to tell you the truth I wasn't all that dead set on becomin' a farmer in the first place. And after what we've been through, and the things we've done over the last few years, I'm not sure I could ever go back to farming."

"It's what pa wanted for us," Will said.

"I know it's what he wanted. But be truthful, Will, is it really what you want?"

Will laughed. "No, it's not what I want. So I have a suggestion."

"What's that?"

"We go back home just long enough to find a buyer for the farm, and we sell it."

"Might be hard to do with the house and the barn burned out."

"We could rebuild the house and the barn," Will suggested. "Or, we could just sell the land. We won't get as much that way, but it won't keep us tied down, either."

"I say sell the land," Gid replied with a broad smile.

Chapter Six

When Will and Gid returned to their old homestead they rode up to the entry gate. The gate had been there since Will and Gid were boys and they knew that Drury had been very proud of it. It arched over the road leading up to the house, and hanging from the arch was a neatly lettered sign.

CROCKETT FARM
Drury, Amanda, William, Gideon
Farmers who wait for perfect weather never plant.
If they watch every cloud, they never harvest.

This Bible verse taken from *Ecclesiastes* was, Will and Gid knew, their father's favorite.

But as the two brothers approached the gate they saw something else, a poster, nailed to the gate.

SHERIFF'S NOTICE
No Trespassing
This land has been confiscated
for non-payment of taxes.

"Damn!" Gid said. "Will, what do you think this means?"

Will sighed. "I'm not sure, but I'm afraid it might mean that we don't have a farm to sell. At least, not until we can pay whatever is owed on it."

"How do we do that?"

"My guess would be that we go into town and find out."

"How much are the taxes?" Will asked the sheriff half an hour later when he and Gid stopped by the office to inquire.

"You mean how much *were* the taxes, don't you?" Sheriff Parker replied. "Because the truth is, it doesn't matter anymore. The land has already been sold."

"We didn't know anything about it."

"You might have found out about it if, after the war ended, you had come home like everyone else did."

"We had some business to attend to," Will said.

"I hope it was important enough business for you to lose your farm."

Will and Gid were quiet for a long moment, then

Will answered for both of them.

"Yeah, it was."

"Well, we didn't want to farm anyway," Gid said when they left the sheriff's office.

"No, but it would have been nice to have been able to sell it, rather than see it taken for taxes," Will replied.

"What do we do now?"

Will smiled. "I suggest we do what we are best at doing."

Two weeks later Will and Gid were waiting on top of a fifteen foot high precipice that was alongside the road that provided stage coach service between Ozark and Buffalo, Missouri. Their horses were tied to a small tree on the ground behind the rock.

"How much money is the coach carrying?" Gid asked.

"Somewhere around a thousand dollars, I would say," Will replied. "It's all the tax money collected from Taney and Ozark Counties."

"I figure they owe us at least that much for taking our farm away from us," Gid said.

"Here it comes," Will said. "Get down so they can't see us against the skyline.

Gid complied and the two men lay down to wait on the approaching coach. As it drew closer they could hear it, the drum of hoof beats from the six horse team, the jangle of bit, bridle, and harness, the roll of the wheels, the rattle and squeak of the coach body in its through braces, and the calls and whistles of the driver.

Win and Gid put hoods over their faces and watched the coach approach, then, just as it passed under them they dropped down onto the top. The attention of the driver and shotgun guard was still directed toward the road in front of them, so neither Will nor Gid were noticed until Will spoke.

"Driver, I wonder if you would be so kind as to stop the team, and ask your messenger to drop his gun."

"What the hell?" the driver said, shocked by the unexpected, "Where did you come from?"

"Oh, here and there," Will replied. "Please do as I say, I don't want to shoot you if I don't have to."

"No, no, don't shoot, we'll do what you say," the driver replied.

"Shotgun?" Gid said.

"Throw the gun aside, Lou," the driver ordered.

As Lou jettisoned his gun, the driver hauled back on the reins and put his foot on the brake, bringing the coach to a halt.

"Order your passengers out of the coach," Will said.

"Mister, you got no need to be goin' after my passengers," the driver said. "They're just innocent folk."

"Order the passengers out," Will said again as he and Gid jumped down to the ground.

"You folks in the coach—everyone out!" the driver shouted.

"What's going on here?" an elderly man said as he climbed out of the coach.

"All of you," Gid said. "Get over there on the side of the road and put your hands up." He reinforced his demand with a little wave of the pistol he was holding.

There were five passengers: the old man, a younger man wearing a suit who had the look of a drummer, a woman and her two children. None of them represented a danger to him.

"Reach down into the boot and hand me down those two money pouches you're carrying," Will ordered.

"What makes you think we're carrying any money at all, let alone two pouches?" the driver asked.

"You are carrying a bank shipment and the revenue receipts. Reach down there and hand them down to us."

The driver lifted two canvas pouches. One of the pouches was marked with the name of the bank, the other pouch read "U.S. Government."

"You can keep this one," Win said, handing the bank pouch back up to the driver. "We'll keep this one."

"Mister, that there money you're a' keepin' belongs to the government," the driver said. "If I was you 'n was only goin' to take one sack, I'd be takin' the bank money. You're goin' to be in a lot more trouble with the government than with the bank."

"It isn't the government's money anymore, it's ours," Will replied in the same conversational tone he had been using for the whole time. "If you two gentlemen would hand us your pistols, we would be most appreciative."

The driver and shotgun guard complied, and Will unloaded both guns, then returned them.

"You folks may return to the coach now," he said.

"Mister, are you'ns real stagecoach robbers?" the young boy asked, excitedly.

"Yes we are, young man. And now you can tell all your friends that you were robbed by a couple of real stagecoach robbers."

"You two should be ashamed of yourselves," the woman scolded.

"Yes, ma'am, sometimes we are," Gid said. "Now please, all of you, climb back into the coach."

Will and Gid watched until the passengers re-boarded, then Will pointed his pistol into the air and fired.

"Heyah!" he shouted, and the team bolted forward.

Shortly after the holdup newspapers in the area, including the *St. Leger Advocate*, carried a story of the stagecoach robbery.

BUFFALO TO OZARK COACH ROBBED

Took Only Tax Receipts

Three days previous, two unknown road agents intercepted the Ozark to Buffalo stagecoach for the purpose of robbing it.

"They were perfect gentlemen about it, I will say that," the driver, Sam Underhill said. "They took nothing from the passengers and they didn't take any of the money that was being transferred by the bank."

Lou Bowman, the messenger guard agreed as to the courteous conduct of the two robbers. As the road agents were wearing hoods not only is their identity unknown, but there is also no description.

There is little taste for hostile feelings for the bandits, because as the bank money was untouched none of the depositors have experienced any loss. And, as many have felt the bite of excessive taxes, there is no sense of sympathy for those who collect the revenue.

The stagecoach holdup netted Will and Gid exactly seven hundred and eighteen dollars. This was less than they would have gotten had they been allowed to sell the farm, but they were pleased with the amount as it would be more than enough to see them through the next two or three months.

They had returned to St. Leger where, eventually both took jobs, Gid in the livery stable and Will as a hostler for a freighting company. They didn't need the money, but took the job so that no one would get curious about their source of income.

Gid had been working at the stable for two months and he was shoveling manure from a stall when he looked up to see Will standing there with a smile on his face.

"Will, what are you doing here? Shouldn't you be at work?"

"I came to ask you a question."

"What question is that?" Gid asked, leaning on his shovel.

"I want to know whether you want to keep shoveling shit, or would you like to come with me?"

"Go with you where?"

"Well, little brother, does it actually matter where we go?"

Gid laughed, and tossed his shovel aside. "No," he said. "It doesn't really matter at all."

"We got a letter from Frank McClain inviting us to Texas," Will said as they were walking away from the stable after Gid gave his notice. "He says that he has found a good project for us if we would go down there and join him."

"Did he say what it is?"

"No, but it has to be better than working in a stable or at a freighting line," Will replied with a little chuckle.

"You got that right. I say we send him a telegram and ask him to meet us at the depot."

"I already have."

"What was the name of that town again?"

"San Saba."

Gid smiled. "San Saba, here we come."

Chapter Seven

San Saba, Texas

"It ain't right, I'm tellin' you. It just ain't right!"

None of the Tanglefoot Saloon patrons were sure who, among their number, made the pronouncement but it was a statement that all, but a few agreed with.

"Hell, if they're goin' to try McCain for fightin' for the South in the war they could try most any of us," another said.

"No, huh-uh, it ain't the same thing. It ain't the same thing at all," another said. "We was most in the regular army, fightin' for generals like Hood, or Bragg, or Hampton. McCain warn't in the regular army; he was one o' them, what they call, guerrillas."

"That don't matter none. He was fightin' for the South, which is what most all of us done."

"Except for the judge and the prosecutor. Both o' them fought for the North 'n they didn't neither one of 'em even come to Texas 'till after the war was over."

"Hey!" someone called from the door of the saloon. "They've opened up the court house, so if anyone wants to watch the trial, you better get over there now!"

At the call nearly everyone in the Tanglefoot hurried out the door, leaving behind only one customer, two bar girls, and the bartender.

"Tucker, you may as well finish your drink," the bartender said to the one remaining customer. "This here bar is about to close."

"What for?"

"What for? Ain't you heard ever' one talkin'? The trial is about to commence 'n I intend to be there when it starts."

Tucker drained the rest of his beer then seeing two more abandoned mugs, he drank those as well.

Even a stranger coming into San Saba would have known something important was about to happen. While most of the stores were either closed, or nearly empty, a significant crowd of people had gathered around the front of the courthouse because there was no room left for them inside.

"Here ye, hear ye, hear ye! This, here trial is about to commence, the Honorable Jacob Hornung, presidin'," the bailiff shouted. "Everybody stand respectful."

The Honorable Jacob Hornung, a short, rotund man with thinning white hair, came out of a back room. After taking his seat at the bench, he adjusted the glasses on the end of his nose, then cleared his throat.

"Would the bailiff please bring the accused before the bench?"

The bailiff, who was leaning against the side wall, spit a quid of tobacco into the brass spittoon, then walked over to the table where the defendant, Frank McCain, sat next to his court-appointed lawyer, Louis Vernia.

"Get up, you," the bailiff growled. "Present yourself before the judge."

Frank was handcuffed, and had shackles on his ankles. He shuffled up to stand in front of the judge. Vernia went with him.

"Frank McCain, you stand accused of the crime of ridin' for that Pearsonin', thievin', rapin' bastard they called Quantrill," the judge said. "How do you plead?"

"Quantrill never raped nobody," Frank said. "It was only the Yankee bastards done that."

"How do you plead?" the judge asked again.

"Your Honor, if it pleases the court," Vernia said.

"You got somethin' to say to this court, Mr. Vernia?" Judge Hornung asked.

"Yes, Your Honor. Quantrill did most of his murderin'

and thievin' up in Kansas and Missouri," the lawyer said.

"What's your point, Mr. Vernia?"

"Well, Your Honor, this is Texas. I don't know why we would be tryin' Mr. McCain in Texas for any murdering and thieving he might have done while he was up in Kansas. I move that this case be dismissed for lack of proper jurisdiction."

"Your Honor, it is known that Quantrill came to Texas once, during the war," the prosecutor said.

"There you go," Judge Hornung said, slapping his gavel on the bench. "If Quantrill was ever down here, even one time, that gives me all the jurisdiction I need."

"But, Your Honor, these were his own people. You know he didn't do any murdering or thieving while he was down here," Vernia said.

"None that we know of, Your Honor," the prosecutor replied quickly. "And I hasten to remind Your Honor we're tryin' this defendant for being one of Quantrill's riders, not for any specific act of murder or robbery he may have done. Therefore, the fact that Quantrill was once in Texas, and that this defendant was with him, puts the case under your jurisdiction."

The judge slapped his gavel on the bench again. "You are right, Mr. Prosecutor. Mr. Vernia, your motion for dismissal is denied. This case shall proceed."

"Your Honor, a moment with my client?" Vernia asked.

"Make it brief."

"McCain, did you come to Texas with Quantrill?"

"Yes and no," McCain replied.

"Yes and no? What does that mean?"

"I came to Texas with him, but wasn't with him while he was here. I took that opportunity to visit with my mother's sister and her family."

"Your Honor," Vernia said then, addressing the court. "While it is true that my client entered Texas at the same time as Quantrill, he spent no time with Quantrill, opting instead to visit with his aunt."

"It doesn't matter whether McCain was physically with Quantrill or not. By his own admission he and Quantrill were in the state of Texas at the same time, and that, counselor for the defense, gives me all the jurisdiction I need to try this case."

"Yes, Your Honor," Vernia said in surrender.

"How do you plead?"

"Your Honor, my client pleads guilty and he throws himself upon the mercy of the court."

"Wait a minute, hold on there!" Frank shouted. "I ain't pleadin' guilty to nothin'!"

The judge glared. "Did you, are did you not, confess before several assembled men in the Tanglefoot Saloon, that you rode with Quantrill?"

"That wasn't what you would call a confession, Judge,"

Frank said. "I didn't have anything to confess. I was just drinkin' and talkin' and tellin' war stories with some of the other fellas, that's all."

"And during the course of your talking, did you say you rode with Quantrill?" the judge asked.

Frank looked at his lawyer. "I don't know much about the law, but ain't there somethin' that says I don't have to answer questions like that?"

"That's right," the lawyer agreed. "It's called the Fifth Amendment, and it says you don't have to answer any question that may incriminate you."

Frank smiled. "That's what I'm goin' to do then. I ain't goin' to answer that question."

"Very well," the judge said. "Clerk, change Mr. McCain's plea from guilty, to not-guilty."

"You're making a big mistake, Mr. McCain," Vernia whispered to him. "I know this judge. If you plead guilty, he might show you some mercy. If you're found guilty, you'll get none."

"Well, what can happen to me? I mean, even if I did ride with Quantrill, what can he do to me besides tell me I can't vote or hold office or something like that? Hell, I never signed no loyalty oath to the goddamn Yankee government, so I can't do none of that anyway."

"Clearly, Mr. McCain, you don't have a grasp of the situation. I'm afraid that the judge can do a lot more than that," Vernia said, ominously.

"What else can he do?"

"He can hang you."

Frank gasped, then put his hand to his throat. "Hang me?" he asked in a choked voice.

"That's right."

Frank looked back up toward the bench. "Judge, I want to change my plea again!"

"Too late for that, boy, we've done entered your plea of not guilty," Judge Hornung said. "Mr. Prosecutor, are you prepared to make your case?"

"I am, Your Honor. You men over there," the prosecutor said, pointing to several men sitting in the front row. "You are all my witnesses. Stand up and hold up your right hand."

The men did as they were instructed, and the clerk swore them in.

"Now," the prosecutor said. "Did all of you hear this man say in the Tanglefoot Saloon that he had ridden for Quantrill?"

All the witnesses nodded yes.

The prosecutor turned back toward the judge. "Well, there you are, Your Honor. Every one of these men have just sworn that they heard the defendant admit to being one of Quantrill's riders durin' the war."

"Mr. Vernia, do you have anything to say in defense

of this wretched soul who is your client?"

"Your Honor, I know that you and the sheriff, and everyone else of authority in this county are Yankees, appointed to office by the Federal Government as part of our reconstruction," Vernia said. "But if you would just look out into the gallery you'll see men and women who were born and raised here. They are good people. Southerners by birth, and during the late unpleasantness they were Southerners by loyalty. If you ask them to pass judgement against a man, simply because he fought for what he believed in, I believe you are going to find that they will think Mr. McCain was just a soldier doing his duty. And as you have come to live among us, I ask that you pass judgement on this matter with some feeling for the sensitivities of those whom you now represent."

The gallery broke into applause at Vernia's statement, and the judge angrily banged his gavel until they were quiet. "I represent the Federal Government of the United States and her laws first," Judge Hornung replied, "and the people and the laws of Texas second." Hornung looked over toward the jury.

"You gentlemen of the jury," he said. "Do you go along with what these folks in the gallery believe? Do you think this man who rode with Quantrill was nothing more than a soldier doing his duty?"

"Your Honor, that's what we think, yes," one of the

men in the jury said after taking a quick, visual poll of his fellow jurors.

"In other words, if you had to make a decision now, you would say not guilty?" the judge asked.

The spokesman for the jury nodded. "Yes, sir, Your Honor, that's what we would say, all right."

Again everyone cheered, and Frank smiled broadly.

"Then you are dismissed," the judge said angrily.

"Thank you, Your Honor," Vernia said, putting his hand on Frank's shoulder.

"No, not the defendant!" the judge said. He pointed to the men in the jury box. "I mean those Rebel bastards on the jury are dismissed. I will decide the case."

"You, your Honor?"

"Do you see any other judge in this room, Mr. Vernia?"

"No, sir."

"Then I will make the decision. In fact, I have already made the decision. Frank McCain, I find you guilty as charged. Now, you stand there, while I administer the sentence."

"Your Honor, we beg for mercy," Vernia said.

Judge Hornung fixed Vernia with an intense scowl as he took off his glasses and began polishing them. Then he looked back at McCain and cleared his throat.

"Frank McCain, you have been tried before me, and you have been found guilty of the crime of riding with the outlaw Quantrill, and aiding and abetting in the atrocities of murder, arson, and robbery that he visited upon innocent people," Judge Hornung said. "Before this court passes sentence, have you anything to say?"

"Judge, all I can say is I was just a soldier, doin' my duty," Frank said. "I know they was lots of Yankee soldiers done just as bad, and some of 'em done worse."

"You were just a soldier doing your duty, you say? Well, Mr. McCain, one day that duty included burning and sacking the town of Lawrence, Kansas. Do you recall that day, sir?"

"Yes, sir, I recall that."

"Were you present on that day?"

Frank cleared his throat. "Yes, Your Honor, I was there that day."

"Lawrence, Kansas was a lovely, peaceful city, Mr. McCain, wherein resided my younger brother, his wife, and two sons. My brother and his two sons were murdered that day. And you, you miserable son of a bitch, whether you personally did it or not, were there when it happened."

Frank looked at the floor then, knowing that there was nothing more he could say, and knowing too that he could expect no mercy from this judge.

"Frank McCain, it is the sentence of this court that you be taken from this courthouse and put in jail. I further direct the constable of this town to build, or cause to be built, a gallows or some other device, fixture, apparatus, contrivance, agent, or whatever means as may be sufficient to suspend your carcass above the ground. When the machine is completed you are to be taken from jail to that contrivance, where you will have a noose placed around your neck. You will then be dropped through a trapdoor, which will bring about the effect of breaking your neck, collapsing your windpipe, and in any and all ways squeezing the last breath of life from your worthless, vile, and miserable body."

"No!" some in the court shouted. "You can't hang him, you Yankee bastard! He ain't guilty of nothin' but bein' a soldier!"

"Constable!" the judge said. "Arrest the man who just made that outburst and hold him in contempt of court!"

The constable stood and looked out over the gallery.

"Arrest which man, Judge?" the constable asked. "I didn't see who it was."

To a man, every person in the courtroom at that moment was quiet.

"Who was it?" the judge asked. "Who made that outburst?"

There was no response to his inquiry.

"All right, all right!" the judge said. "You Rebel bastards think you are putting one over on me. But we'll see who has the last laugh when this miserable bastard is hanged. Constable, I leave the prisoner in your hands. You are to watch over him until the sentence is carried out."

"Yes, sir," the constable said.

"In the meantime I had best hurry down to the depot and catch the train when it returns to Lampasas."

The judge, the sheriff, and the bailiff hurried out the back door then, leaving the courtroom under the control of the city constable. Unlike the three officers of the court, Constable Biddle was a native Texan and personally sympathetic to the lost cause of the South.

"Goddamn, Biddle, you ain't goin' to actual hang this boy, are you?" someone called.

"You heard the judge, Herbert," Biddle replied. "He give me the order. There ain't nothin' I can do about it."

"Son of a bitch! Hangin' a man just 'cause he soldiered for the wrong side. That ain't right!"

"Come on, Vernia," the constable said. "You've got to help me get this prisoner back into jail."

The crowd booed, and shouted angry curses at the constable and the lawyer as they began escorting Frank back to the jail cell. But though the mood of the crowd was ugly, they made no attempt to try and rescue Frank McCain.

Chapter Eight

Gideon Crockett was walking behind a mule, watching the dirt fold away from the plowshare as it opened a deep, new furrow. A few yards in front of him his older brother, Will, was plowing another furrow; while a few yards behind, their father was breaking open a third row. Half the field had already been tilled and the coal-black dirt glistened with the nutrients that made the soil so fertile.

Gid looked over toward the two-story white house where he had grown up, and at the barn, granary, and machine shed that made up the Crockett farm. The windows in the house were shining brightly in the sunlight first silver, then gold, then red. The color spread from the windows to the side of the house, then to the roof, and then to the other buildings. But as the color intensified, Gid was shocked to see that it wasn't reflected sunlight at all.

It was fire!

The house, barn, and all the outbuildings were engulfed in a blazing inferno!

Gid looked back toward his father and gasped, for his father was now a human torch. Flames were leaping up from his body, yet he continued to walk behind the plow, as if totally unconcerned that he was being consumed by fire.

"Will! Will!" Gid shouted.

"I'm right here, Gid," Will's calm voice answered.

Gid looked up with a start and saw his brother's concerned face. Now, outside sounds intruded...the rattle and squeak of a train in motion, the rhythmic clicking of wheels over track joints, the conversations of other passengers. Time and place returned and he realized that this wasn't pre-war Missouri, this was post-war Texas.

"Are you all right?" Will asked.

Gid ran his hand across his face, as if wiping the sleep away. "Yeah," he answered. He sat up. "Yeah, I'm all right."

"Did you have that dream again?"

Gid nodded without speaking.

"Gid, there wasn't anything we could have done," Will reminded him. "Hoffman came to the farm while we were gone. They killed Ma and Pa and burned the place. You've got to get over feelin' guilty about it."

"If we hadn't stopped for a drink, if we had gone straight home, it wouldn't have happened," Gid said.

"It wasn't just you wanted to stop for a drink," Will reminded him. "I was with you, remember? And I wanted a drink as much as you. Besides, that was a long time ago."

"Yeah, I know it was a long time ago."

"And we just took care of the son of a bitch who did it," Will said.

Despite the grief he had been experiencing just a moment earlier, Gid smiled. "Yeah," he said. "Yeah, we did, didn't we?"

"I don't know why this has been bothering you so much lately. You didn't have these dreams during the war. And don't forget, little brother, we did our own share of burning and killing."

"Yeah, I guess we did."

With Gid at ease over his dream, Will looked out the window and saw nothing but mesquite and dirt sliding by under the late afternoon sun. He didn't believe he had ever seen anything as God-awful-ugly as West Texas.

The view inside wasn't all that attractive either. It consisted mostly of overweight drummers and washed-out, poor immigrant families. It had improved somewhat when a young woman had gotten on the train a couple of hours earlier. When she'd boarded, she'd smiled at Will while passing by, looking for a seat.

Somewhat later a young, sandy-haired cowboy, wearing an ivory-handled pistol, leather chaps, and highly polished silver rowels, had gotten on the train. He'd swaggered back and forth through the car a few times before finally settling in a seat next to the pretty young woman.

Will looked back out the window at the passing scenery. A few minutes later when Will looked toward the woman and the cowboy, he saw that though they were still together, the young woman did not appear to be enjoying the cowboy's company. She got up and changed seats, but it was to no avail, as the cowboy also changed seats to be near her. The young woman got up again, and this time she stepped out onto the vestibule. The cowboy waited for a moment, then got up as well and followed her outside.

Will turned his attention away from the two. "Where are we, anyway?" he asked.

"We're nearly there. I just heard the conductor say we'd be coming into San Saba in a few minutes," Gid answered.

"Frank says he has a deal that is too sweet for us to pass up. I wonder what it is," Will said.

"Frank was always pretty dependable, remember? When he came back with a scouting report, we could always count on it being good information," Gid said.

"That's true," Will agreed. He stretched, then stood up. "I think I'm going to step out onto the vestibule and get a breath of air."

"Don't fall off," Gid quipped.

Will smiled, and picked his way forward through the rattling, rocking car. When he stepped outside he saw that the pretty young woman was still being pursued by the cowboy.

"Please," the girl was saying. "Please, just leave me alone."

"Who do you think you're foolin', by bein' so high-and-mighty?" the cowboy asked. "I know who you are, and I know what you are."

"I am someone who wants to be left alone," the woman said.

Will looked over toward them to measure the sincerity in the woman's voice. He was hesitant to butt into anyone else's business, but the woman was clearly having a hard time with this cowboy

"Mister, why don't you go away and leave the lady alone?" Will asked.

The cowboy looked toward Will as if shocked that anyone would have the audacity to butt in.

"What did you just say to me?"

"I told you to leave the lady alone."

"Why don't you just go to Hell?" the cowboy growled menacingly. He turned back to the girl, as if dismissing Will out of hand. Will stepped across the gap between them and grabbed the cowboy by the scruff of the neck and the seat of his pants.

"Hey, what the…" the cowboy shouted, but whatever the fourth word was going to be was lost in the rattle of cars and the cowboy's own surprised scream as Will threw the young man off the train. The cowboy hit on the down-slope of the track base, then bounced and rolled through the rocks and scrub-weed alongside the train. Will leaned out far enough to see him stand up and shake his fist, but by then the train had swept on away from him.

"He'll be all right," Will said. "He'll have a little walk into town, is all."

The girl laughed, and even above the sound of the train Will could hear the musical lilt to her laugh. Gid stepped out onto the platform at that moment.

"What is it?" Gid asked. "What happened?"

"The fella with all the silver just got off the train," Will said easily. He looked at the girl. "Do you know him?"

"Yes. His name is Glasscock. Lee Glasscock. He works for Hector Laroche."

"I never stopped to think that you might know him. I hope I wasn't out of line. I hope you were serious when you told him to leave you alone."

"I was very serious, and you weren't out of line at all," she said.

The train started slowing.

"This is it," Gid said. "Our stop."

"Oh!" the girl said. "You're getting off here?"

"Yes, ma'am," Will answered.

"So am I. Maybe we'll see each other again," she suggested hopefully.

Will smiled, and touched the brim of his hat. "You can count on it."

"Come on, big brother," Gid said. "We have to see to our horses."

Some fifteen minutes later, Will and Gid had their horses off the stock car and saddled as the train, its whistle blowing, bell ringing, and steam puffing, started chugging away from the depot.

As the noise of the receding train faded, it was replaced by the sound of hammering and sawing.

"Sounds like some building goin' on," Will said. "Must be a busy little town."

"Frank said it was," Gid said. "By the way, where is he? I thought he was going to meet us."

"Yeah, so did I. But I sure as hell don't see him."

"So, what do we do now?"

"Maybe he had to go somewhere. Best thing for us to do is board our horses, get us a room in the hotel, then wait around a few days."

As Will was talking, the young woman he had rescued on the train walked by. She nodded in his direction, then smiled again.

Gid chuckled. "From the looks of things, waitin' around may not be all that hard for you," he suggested.

"We do what we can, little brother, to while away the hours," Will teased.

The two brothers mounted and started toward the stable. When they reached the street side of the depot, they saw the cause of the construction sounds they had been hearing. At the far end of the street, a gallows was being built.

"I'll be damned," Gid said. "Look at that. I wonder who it's for?"

"Why don't we ride down there and ask?"

There were two carpenters up on the platform itself, and a third down on the ground, sawing boards at a sawhorse. Half a dozen young boys, barefooted and with ragged bottoms to their pants, stood around watching.

"You boys get away from here," a large, middle-aged man shouted to the youngsters. "This ain't no place for you. What are you doin' out here, anyway? Your mamas will be setting supper to the table soon."

"We want to see the hangin'," one of the boys answered.

"Well, there ain't goin' to be no hangin' today, so why don't you go on. Get away and let these men get their work done!"

The man who was shouting was wearing a badge. He

looked up at Will and Gid, and as they were mounted, the action caused him to have to look into the brightness of the sky behind them. He squinted.

"Don't know you two fellas, do I?" he asked.

"We just came in on the train," Gid answered.

"So it's already started, has it?"

"I beg your pardon?" Will asked. "What's already started?"

"Folks comin' in to see the hangin'. Well I'll tell you just like I told these kids. The hangin' ain't until tomorrow."

"You the sheriff?" Will asked.

"I'm the town constable. The name's Biddle. Walt Biddle. Used to be sheriff of San Saba County, but I wouldn't swear no oath of loyalty to the goddamn Yankee government, so I can't be sheriff no more." He spat a quid of tobacco, then wiped the residue from his chin with the back of his hand.

Will nodded toward the gallows. "Truth is, we didn't know anything about the hangin'. It's tomorrow, you say?"

"The lynchin' takes place tomorrow afternoon at two o'clock."

Curious at Biddle's remark, Will twisted in his saddle for another look at the gallows.

"Lynching? Never heard of building' a gallows for a lynching," he said. "Always thought they used something like a stout tree limb, or a telegraph pole, for things like that.

"Yeah, well, you might call this hangin' a *legal* lynchin'. It's legal 'cause they was a trial, if you can call what they had for this fella a trial."

"You sayin' he didn't get a fair trial?"

"Ain't my place to say," Biddle answered.

"Sure it is. You're an officer of the law, aren't you?"

"I told you, I'm just the town constable. The real law around here belongs to Hector Laroche."

"Hector Laroche?"

"You know him?"

"I'm not sure," Will answered. He remembered the girl telling him that the cowboy he threw off the train worked for Hector Laroche. "I believe I've heard that name somewhere before. It's the second time I've heard it today. Who is he?"

"He was some Yankee bigwig during the war," Biddle answered. "They say he was a general, but I don't know if he was a fightin' general."

Will snapped his fingers. "The Kansas Tenth," he said. "I *have* heard of him. He was their general, but he never actually rode with them."

"That's him, all right."

"What's he doing down here, in Texas?"

"He come down here after the war with a carpetbag full of government warrants and bills, and he's turned

77

all them Yankee laws into Yankee dollars."

"Sounds like a fella could get rich doing that," Gid suggested.

"He's rich enough to buy up half the land in the county."

"And the law?" Will asked.

Biddle nodded. "And the law."

"It's just a guess, Constable, but I'd say he hasn't bought you," Will said.

Biddle snorted. "Hell, what would the son of a bitch want with me? I ain't worth his money. I don't do nothin' more'n run away pesky kids, or now and again I might throw a drunk in jail to sleep it off."

"This fella they're hangin' tomorrow. Are they keeping him in your jail?" Will asked.

Biddle nodded. "Yeah, a man by the name of Frank McCain. You ever heard of him?"

Will and Gid exchanged a quick, secretive look.

"Uh, no, we've never heard of him," Will replied. "What did he do?"

"Do? Hell, he didn't do nothin' but get drunk the other night and tell some folks he once rode with Quantrill. Seems like our sheriff and judge have a special hatred for anyone who ever rode with Quantrill. They've got ever' poster ever put out on any of 'em, includin' some, I think, that was put out durin' the war. Truth is, most of those wanted posters wouldn't be given a second look in any other county but San Saba. Makes no difference to our judge and sheriff, though. If a man rode for Quantrill, he'd be a lot better off if he'd just stay away from here."

"I don't understand that. This bein' a Southern town, why would your judge and sheriff have such a special hatred for Quantrill's men?" Gid asked.

"'Cause there ain't neither one of them is Southerners. They was both appointed to their offices down here. The Judge was a lawyer somewhere up in Kansas and the sheriff was a first sergeant in the Tenth Kansas."

"Laroche's division?" Will asked.

"Now you're beginning to catch on," Biddle said. "The judge and the sheriff come down here with Laroche and the other carpetbaggers. Just like buzzards, they've started pickin' the carcass clean. By now, they've pretty near taken over all of West Texas…stealin' land for back taxes and buying up businesses for pennies on the dollar."

"What do the locals think of it?"

"The real folk—that is, the decent folk in this town—still have a lot of hard feelings against the Yankees, especially them that have come down here to take over things. And if you'd ask one of them, they'd likely tell you that Quantrill, Bloody Bill Anderson, and others like them was patriots, and Frank McCain and them that rode with Quantrill was brave men."

"Glad to hear that," Will said.

"You boys wasn't with Quantrill, was you?" Biddle held up his hand almost as soon as he asked the question. "No," he said. "Don't answer that. It'd be better all around. But unless I miss my guess, you two was in the war yourselves."

"Yes," Will said.

"You don't sound Texan though. More like Arkansas, or Missouri," Biddle said.

"Could be either one," Gid said.

"I'd be careful 'bout who I told that to. Quantrill was in Missouri."

"So was Sterling Price, General Van Dorn, Jo Shelby, Jeff Thompson, and several others," Will replied.

"What do you say we just let it go at that?" Biddle suggested.

"I'd say that was a good idea." Will said.

"You boys plannin' on staying around for a while?"

"A couple of days maybe. I see the Tanglefoot across the street. Is that a pretty good place to wet a whistle?"

"If you don't mind givin' your money to General Laroche," Biddle said. "If you're more partial to a Southern patriot, you might try Sam's Place, just up the street a ways. His whiskey ain't watered and he's a good man."

"Thanks," Will said, touching the brim of his hat and turning his mount away.

"What are we goin' to do about Frank, Will?" Gid asked quietly as they rode away.

"Don't know as there's anything we can do about it," Will replied.

"I hate to just stand by and watch him hang."

"We're on the wrong side of the law, little brother. When you're on this side, hangin' is a risk we all take."

Instinctively, Gid reached up to pull his shirt collar away from his neck.

Chapter Nine

Will and Gid put their horses up at the livery, then walked across the street to the saloon known as Sam's Place. It was not yet supper time, and a little early for peak business, so the saloon was only about one-third full. The scarred piano sat unused in the back of the room. There were two saloon girls working the customers, but they were occupied by a table full of men.

"Two beers," Will ordered, sliding a piece of silver across the bar. The man behind the bar drew two mugs and set them, with foaming heads, in front of the brothers. They drank the first ones down without taking away the mug. Then they wiped the foam away from their lips and slid the empty mugs back toward the barkeep.

"That one was for thirst," Will explained. "This will be for taste. Do it again."

Smiling, the bartender gave them a second round.

With the beer in his hand, Will turned his back to the bar and looked out over the saloon. Noticing them then, one of the two girls pulled herself away from the table and sidled up to the two brothers. She had bleached hair and was heavily painted, but behind her tired eyes was a suggestion of good humor. She smiled at Gid.

"What a handsome devil you are," she said. "I'll just bet you've broken many a poor girl's heart."

"I've bent them around a few times," Gid quipped. "Don't know as I ever broke any."

The girl laughed. "My name's Florrie," she said. "What's yours?"

"Gid." Gid turned toward the bartender. "It looks to me like this lovely young lady needs a drink."

"Coming right up," the bartender said, filling a glass from Florrie's special bottle.

It was at that moment that the bat-wing doors swung open, and the cowboy in black and silver came in. He had scratches and bruises on his face, and his clothes were dirty and torn.

"You lost, Glasscock? This ain't the Tanglefoot," someone said.

Glasscock glared at the speaker, and that was when everyone noticed his condition.

"What the hell happened to you?" someone asked.

"Some son of a bitch pushed me off the train," Glasscock growled.

Everyone laughed.

Glasscock started to say something else, then saw Will standing quietly at the bar, calmly drinking his beer. He pointed his finger at him.

"You!" he shouted. He was so choked with anger that he could barely get the words out. "You're the one who did this to me!"

"Did you have a nice walk into town, Glasscock?" Will asked easily. He took another swallow of his beer, then pulled the mug back down and wiped the back of his hand across his mouth. "Why don't you have a beer on me? You could probably use one."

"You son of a bitch! You offer me a beer? You offer me a beer and think I'll forget about what you did to me? What the hell got into you, mister, to do a damn thing like that?"

"Back where I come from, when a lady asks a man to leave, he does," Will said. "Since you didn't leave when she asked you, I figured maybe you could use a little lesson in manners."

Again everyone laughed.

"Is that what this is all about, Glasscock? Teaching you some manners?" someone asked.

"We'll see who is the teacher and who is the pupil around here," Glasscock said. "I'm going to teach this bastard never to butt into anyone else's business again."

He grinned evilly. "Only the lesson ain't goin' to do him no good, 'cause he's going to be dead. Pull your gun, mister! Pull your gun! I'm goin' to shoot your eyes out, now!"

The laughter stopped then. This had gone beyond joking and, anticipating a killing, there was a quick scrape of chairs and tables as everyone, including Florrie, scrambled to get out of the way.

Gid was the only one who didn't move away from Will.

"Looks like he doesn't want your beer," Gid said nonchalantly.

"I reckon not."

"I'll take it then," Gid said calmly. He looked back toward the barkeep, who had ducked down behind the bar.

"Oh, there you are," he said easily. "Could I have another beer, please?"

"Mister, are you crazy?" the barkeep hissed up at him. He was waving for Gid to get away. "You'd better get out of the line of fire!"

"What line of fire?" Gid asked innocently.

"Didn't you just hear what Glasscock said? He's going to commence shootin'!"

Gid chuckled, then looked around toward Glasscock, who was standing about twenty feet away, his arm crooked and his hand opening and closing nervously just above the handle of his pistol.

"You're not talking about that little pissant standing

over there, are you?" Gid asked calmly.

"Oh, my, you shouldn't have said that," the bartender said in a frightened voice.

"Hell, mister, there's no call for you to be worryin' about him. We're not in any line of fire. As soon as he twitches, Will will kill him. Now, how about that beer?"

"Beer?" the bartender repeated, as if unable to believe Gid's total lack of concern for what was happening.

"Yes, and listen," Gid went on, as if the next beer was much more important than the impending gun battle. "When you draw my beer this time, could you tip the mug a little so there isn't quite as much foam? I swear, that last one was mostly head."

Several people gasped. They were as surprised as the bartender by Gid's easy words and calm manner.

The barkeep didn't move.

"What about it? Do you get me another beer, or do I have to draw it myself?"

Raising himself just far enough to take the mug, the bartender quickly drew another beer, then set it on the bar and ducked down again.

"Thanks," Gid said. He blew the foam off, then turned around. He was still standing right next to Will, clearly in the line of fire if a gunfight should break out. He took a swallow of his beer and stared across the room at Glasscock.

Glasscock, like the others, had heard Gid's calm declaration. It was beginning to have an effect on him, and his hands started shaking.

"Look at the little sonofabitch shake," Gid said. "Hell, you might as well go ahead and kill him and get it over with, big brother. Otherwise he's goin' to stand right there and piss in his pants."

"You're right," Will said. "All right, Glasscock, let's do it."

"No!" Glasscock suddenly screamed, holding his hands up. "No, I'm not going to draw on you!" He turned to face the others. "You are all my witnesses! I'm not going to fight!"

"If you aren't going to fight, and you won't take my beer, then I suggest that you get the hell out of here," Will growled.

Glasscock licked his lips a couple of times, then turned and ran outside, chased out into the street by the laughter of everyone in the saloon.

"Step up to the bar, boys!" someone shouted. "The drinks are on the house! Anytime I can see one of Laroche's boys backed down like that, it's worth a round."

"Beer!"

"Whiskey!"

More than a dozen voices called out their orders as everyone rushed to the bar. The man who had offered to buy the drinks came down from the stairs where he had been a witness to what just transpired. He walked over to Will and Gid with his hand extended and a broad smile on his lips.

"Sam Eubanks is the name. You two boys are new around here, aren't you?"

"Just got off the train," Will said.

"Yes, I heard about the incident on the train with Mr. Glasscock." Sam took in the saloon with an expansive sweep of his long arm. "I own this place ... and you are as welcome as rain. Especially after what you did for Katie."

"Katie?"

"The girl you rescued on the train," Sam said.

"She works here?"

"In a manner of speaking, she does. She's my daughter," Sam said. He pointed toward the back of the saloon and there, coming down the stairs, was the same young woman Will had seen on the train. She smiled as she walked toward them.

"Hello," Katie said. "We were not formerly introduced on the train. I think my father told you, my name is Katie."

"I'm Will and this is my brother, Gid."

"It's so nice to meet you," Katie said.

"Are you two boys staying in town?" Sam asked.

"For a short time," Will said.

"Far as I'm concerned, you two can stay for as long as you want. But I have to warn you that you've made a dangerous enemy, today. And he has dangerous friends."

"'Won't be the first time we've made enemies," Will replied.

Sam laughed. "No, I'm sure it isn't."

"Say, Sam, where might be a good place to eat around here?"

"I'd recommend Benji's, right next door," Sam answered. "Tell you what. You two go over there and eat all you want. Tell Benji to put it on my tab."

"That's mighty decent of you," Gid said. "Will, what do you say we go have some supper? I could eat a horse."

"Don't say that around Benji," Florrie teased, coming back up to stand beside Gid. "You never know but what he might take you up on it."

Those close enough to overhear her laughed.

Gid looked at Florrie. "Will you be here when I come back?"

"Honey, in case you ain't noticed it, you've done got my comb red," Florrie said. "I'll be here waitin' for you, just anytime you're ready."

Florrie's directness caused Gid to take a quick breath.

"On second thought, Will, why don't you go on over there without me?" he suggested.

"I thought you were so all-fired ready to have supper," Will said.

"Yeah, well, I think I'd rather have another drink with

this young lady."

"All right. I guess I can eat by myself."

"You don't have to eat by yourself, Mr. Crockett," Katie said. "Unless you'd rather not be bothered with a foolish girl's company."

Will smiled. "Well, now, if I turned down the offer of such beautiful company, *I'd* be the fool," he said. "I'd be pleased and honored to have you eat with me." He offered Katie his arm.

The china, silver, and glass gleamed softly in the reflected light of more than a dozen lanterns. Benji's Restaurant was an oasis of light in the darkness that had descended over the little town.

"The Laroche ranch takes up most of the county," Katie was explaining as she ate with Will. "Laroche Ranch is now made up of what used to be Paradise, the A Bar A, Brush Creek, and a couple of other, smaller ranches. I was born on Brush Creek. It belonged to my father."

"I didn't realize your father was a rancher."

"He was a rancher and so was my grandfather before him. When Laroche took over Brush Creek, he got a ranch that had been thriving since Texas was part of Mexico."

"I don't understand. If the ranch was doing that well, why did you father sell out to Laroche?"

Katie looked up sharply. "My father didn't sell Brush

Creek," she said. "He had it stolen from him. Not one penny did he get for it."

"How can that be?"

"Laroche got Brush Creek the same way he got Paradise and all the other ranches. He paid the taxes and took over the property. Only in my father's case, he didn't even know there were any taxes due. Laroche took the taxes off the books and paid them before the notices were even sent out."

"But how could he get away with something like that?" Will asked. "Where was the law?"

"Laroche *is* the law. You have to remember that none of our officials actually represent the people now. They have all been appointed to their positions by the people in Washington. We lost the war, Mr. Crockett, and the Yankees are seeing to it that we pay for it."

"I ran across the constable when I came into town," Will said. "Walt Biddle, I think he said his name was. He mentioned that he used to be the sheriff."

Katie smiled. "Uncle Walt was sheriff for fifteen years."

"Uncle Walt?"

"My mother's brother," Katie explained. "He found out what Laroche was doing with the taxes, and he started going around the county warning people. Laroche got wind of it, and had the Yankees push Uncle Walt out of office."

"I believe he told me he wouldn't take the loyalty oath," Will said.

Katie smiled. "Laroche knew that he would never take the oath, and he knew that was all it would take to get rid of him. So he had his cronies come down here and make Uncle Walt an offer. Either take the oath and help in the administration of the law, which meant evict people from the homes and ranches they and their parents before them had built, or refuse to take the oath and give up the office. Uncle Walt chose to give up the office, but I wish he would have taken it. The whole county was a lot better off when he was sheriff."

"He can't help anyone as constable?"

Katie shook her head. "He has no authority to do anything. Laroche's hand-picked sheriff stops him, every time he tries."

"That's him, right over there," a loud voice suddenly said.

Will looked toward the front door and saw Lee Glasscock pointing at him. The man Glasscock was talking to was a tall, broad-shouldered man with a sweeping handlebar moustache. He was wearing a badge.

"Is that the sheriff?" Will asked.

"Sheriff Felix Martin," Katie said.

"Felix Martin?"

"Yes. Have you heard of him?"

"Indeed, I have," Will said, remembering that Felix Martin was one of the two men he and Gid had been looking for.

"I don't know what you have heard about him," Katie said quietly. "But I can tell you this. He's as mean a man as ever kicked a dog."

Chapter Ten

All eyes in the restaurant were on the sheriff as he walked over to the table where Will and Katie were eating. Will got up from the table and wiped his mouth with a napkin before he turned toward the sheriff. It was a casual move, but one that cleared the way for Will to pull his gun quickly if need be. The move wasn't lost on Martin, who halted for just a step or two before continuing on.

"Something I can do for you, Sheriff?" Will asked.

"What's your name?" the sheriff asked.

"My name is Will Crockett." Will smiled, disarmingly. "And you must be Sheriff Martin I've heard so much about."

Martin stroked his chin with his forefinger. "You look familiar to me, Mr. Crockett. We ever run acrosst each other afore?"

"I doubt it. I just arrived in town today."

"Wasn't talkin' about here. I was talkin' about before,"

Martin said.

"Could be," Will answered. "I've traveled around quite a bit since the war. I figure you have too, seein' as that's no Texas accent."

"Kansas," Martin answered. "And yours is what? Missouri?"

"Arkansas, but lots of times folks get us all mixed up. I reckon it's them Ozark hills. Makes us all sound the same." Will exaggerated his Ozark twang.

Martin nodded toward Glasscock, who hadn't advanced beyond the door. "This fella says you pushed him off the train. Did you?"

"No."

"What?" Glasscock shouted, his voice practically going into falsetto. "Sheriff Martin, he's lying!"

Martin stroked his chin again, and studied Will for a moment. "Now, let me get this straight. You're saying you did *not* push Lee Glasscock off the train?"

"That's what I'm saying."

"Look at him. He's bruised and cut, his clothes are dirty and torn. How do you reckon he got that way?"

"I think it happened when he fell off," Will said. "I saw him start to fall and reached out to grab him, but it was too late." Will smiled. "Now that I think about it, he must've seen me reach for him. Why, Sheriff, I'll just bet that's why he thinks I pushed him."

"You *did* push me!"

"Mr. Crockett is telling the truth, Sheriff," Katie said. "I was on the train too, and I saw the whole thing."

"You're lying! Both of you!" Glasscock sputtered in frustrated anger.

"Glasscock," Will said coldly. "I'd think twice about calling a lady a liar if I were you."

"Crockett, I don't intend to let you start anything in here," Martin said quickly.

"I'm not planning on starting anything, Sheriff," Will said. "But I'll damn sure finish it."

Martin looked at Will for a long moment, then turned to Glasscock. "Glasscock, it looks to me like you fell off the train. Try and be more careful from now on."

"But..." Glasscock said.

"Go on back out to the ranch," the sheriff told him. "If you stay in town you're going to get yourself in trouble."

Defeated, Glasscock turned and left the restaurant.

Martin went with him, but just before he exited, he stopped long enough to let his eyes sweep around the room, taking in all the diners, as if making a mental note for future reference as to who was here.

Martin's exit was followed by a collective sigh of relief from all. Then there was a sudden buzz of excited voices as everyone tried to talk at once. Whatever the subject of conversations had been before Sheriff Martin came into the room, they had all changed. Now everyone was talking about what they had just seen.

"Thanks for backing me up," Will said to Katie. "Under the circumstances, lying seemed the best way to go." He laughed. "And you have to admit, my denying it did about give Mr. Glasscock conniptions."

Katie put her hand across the table and rested it on Will's arm. "Watch out for Sheriff Martin, Will," she said. "He is not the kind you would want to turn your back on."

"Thanks for the warning," Will said.

At that same moment, in the dark street just in front of the restaurant, Glasscock and Sheriff Martin were talking.

"I can't believe you let the son of a bitch get away with lying like that," Glasscock growled. "You should've done something about it."

"What could I do about it? The girl backed him up."

"She was lying too."

"She said it in front of the entire restaurant," Martin said. "Even if I had arrested him, when it came to a court hearing, it would be their word against yours."

"I thought you had some loyalty to General Laroche."

"I've proven my loyalty to the general many times," Martin said. "I don't have to prove any loyalty to you."

"Sergeant Martin, you forget I was a lieutenant and—"

"It's *Sheriff* Martin now, Glasscock. And I haven't

forgotten anything. I had to go along with it during the war 'cause you was duly appointed over me—and because you are the general's nephew. But the war's over and you don't outrank me anymore. In fact, you ain't jack-shit now, and I don't intend to waste my time wiping the snot off your nose ever' time you bite off more'n you can chew."

"If you're talkin' about that McCain fella that I got into it with the other night, I coulda handled him. I didn't ask you to arrest him."

"You could've handled him? He was half an inch away from killin' you. It's a good thing we're hangin' him to-morrow. Otherwise he'd be comin' after you."

"All right, so maybe I did let the argument get a little out of hand. At least I got him to admit that he was a bush-whacker, didn't I? I mean, if he hadn't started braggin' about ridin' with Quantrill, you would've never known."

"That's right. I would've never known."

"So, now, what about Crockett? What are you going to do about him?"

"I'm not going to do anything about him."

"Sergeant, you can't just—" Glasscock began but Martin held up his index finger and shook it back and forth. "I mean, Sheriff," Glasscock corrected. "You can't just do nothing."

"The hell I can't. If you have a problem with Crockett, take care of it yourself."

"All right," Glasscock said. His eyes narrowed. "All right, I will. But when it happens, you just remember that it was your idea."

"When what happens?" Martin scoffed as he mounted his horse. "Crockett would shoot you down before you even cleared leather."

"How do you know?"

"Because I know him."

"You know him?"

"Not him personally, but I know his kind." Martin knew that the Crocketts were after him, but he wasn't ready to share that information. "His soul died during the war. What's left is nothing but pure hate and venom. His kind is going to kill until he gets killed, and it don't matter that much to him which way it comes out." Martin clucked at his horse and began to ride away.

"Yeah, well, he doesn't look so tough to me!" Glasscock called after him. "You just watch me and see! I'll handle him!"

Glasscock looked back toward Benji's Restaurant. Crockett had now made a fool of him three times. Once on the train, once in the saloon, and once in the restaurant. Three times! He was not going to let that happen again. Whatever it took, he was going to make things right with Mr. Crockett. He looked down the dark street toward Martin. "And when I settle with Mr.

Crockett, I may just have an accounting with *you*," he said under his breath.

Will and Katie had just finished eating, and were about to leave the restaurant, when Gid came in.

"So, how was supper?" Gid asked, his words jaunty, his mood ebullient.

"Well, little brother, you certainly look bright-eyed and bushy-tailed."

"Do I? Well, a little lady named Florrie and I had some very pleasant business to attend to."

"So it appears. I'm glad to see that you decided to take the time to eat," Will teased. "You are going to eat, aren't you?"

"Yes, right now eating sounds like a pretty good idea," Gid replied.

"Try the steak, it's very good."

"Reckon I'll just try two steaks," Gid replied.

Will laughed, then held the door open for Katie as they went outside.

"You and your brother seem to get along very well," she said.

"Yes."

"That's good. I think family should be close. What about the rest of your family? Any other brothers, sisters? Where do your parents live?"

"Gid and I are all that's left," Will said. "Our mother and father were killed during the war. Jayhawkers."

Katie put her hand on Will's arm. "Oh, Will, I'm sorry," she said.

"It was several years ago," Will said. He didn't add that the local sheriff was one of the men who had been there that day. He and Gid had come in response to Frank's letter to get into something good. What Frank hadn't said, and what was a fortuitous bonus of their trip down here was that they had located Felix Martin.

The town of San Saba was actually two towns, divided by the railroad track. The north side of the track was the American side, while the Mexican population was concentrated on the south side.

Rip-sawed lumber buildings made up the American town, while across the tracks, adobe buildings were laid out around a dusty plaza.

Lee Glasscock crossed over to the south side of the tracks, then tied his horse off at a hitch rail in front of Antonio's Cantina. A woman's high, clear voice was singing, and it and the accompanying guitar music spilled out through the beaded doorway.

Although Glasscock knew that the Mexicans were generally much poorer than the Americans, you couldn't tell that by listening. The cantina was buzzing with energetic conversation, and bubbling over with laughter.

Glasscock pushed through the hanging beads. He was sure he could find a solution to his problem inside.

Katie and her father lived on the top floor of the saloon, and it was a walk of no more than a few dozen steps from the restaurant to Sam's Place. Will escorted her home, then told her good-bye and started down the street to the hotel to get a room for himself and his brother.

It was very dark outside. There were no street lamps in this small town so that only the moon and a few dim squares of light splashing through open windows kept it from being as black as the inside of a pit. At the far end of the street, however, Will could see the gruesome shape of the gallows. It was dimly illuminated by the moon, and by a splash of light which fell from the front window of the jail house.

The piano player, who had been absent when Will was in the saloon earlier, was hard at work now, an empty beer mug sitting on top in the hope that there would be a few generous patrons. Now his rendition of "Lorena" spilled out into the street from Sam's Place.

From the shadows of the Mexican quarters on the south side of the tracks Will could hear a guitar and trumpet. They were playing different songs, yet somehow it all seemed to blend into a single melody.

A dog barked.

Somewhere a baby cried.

Will saw the lights of the hotel and started toward them.

He felt the assassins coming for him before he heard them, and he heard them before he saw them. Two men suddenly jumped from the dark shadows between the buildings, making wide slashes with their knives. Only that innate sense which allowed him to perceive danger when there was no other sign saved his life, for he was moving out of the way at the exact moment the two men were starting their attacks. Otherwise their knives, swinging in low, vicious arcs, would have disemboweled him.

Despite the quickness of his reaction, however, one of the knives did manage to cut him, and as Will went down into the dirt, rolling to get away from them, the flashing blade opened up a long wound in his side. The knife was so sharp and wielded so adroitly that Will barely felt it. He knew, however, that the knife had drawn blood.

But for all their skill with the blades, the assassins had made a bad mistake. Both were wearing white *peon* shirts and trousers, so that despite the darkness of the street, they were easy to see. And being easy to see, they were easy to avoid.

One of the assassins moved in quickly, thinking to

finish Will off before he could recover. But Will twisted around on the ground, then thrust his feet out, catching the assailant in the chest with a powerful kick and driving him back several feet. The other one darted in then, his action keeping Will off his feet and away from his gun.

The assailants were good, skilled and agile. Will sent a booted foot whistling toward one of them, catching the man in the groin. Then he lunged upward, and rammed stiff fingers to gouge the other in both eyes.

"Aiiyee!" the assailant screamed, dropping his knife and reaching up to his face.

The one who had been kicked in the groin reached for his partner and, pulling him away, broke off the fight. The two men ran toward the track, then disappeared into the darkness on the other side before Will managed to get a good look at their faces. He knew only that they were Mexicans, but he didn't know why they had attacked him.

Will felt the nausea beginning to rise. Bile surged to his throat. Light-headed now, he turned and staggered back down the road toward the saloon. He grabbed the porch pillar for support and pulled himself up onto the plank porch, then pushed in through the door to stand in the brightness.

One of the bar girls happened to be looking toward the door just as he came in, and seeing the bloody apparition standing there, screamed.

All conversation stopped at Will's entrance, and a dead silence hung over the saloon as if it were something palpable. Everyone stared at him, their eyes wide and their mouths open in shock.

Will didn't realize it, but he was terrifying to behold. He was standing just inside the doorway, ashen-faced and holding his hand over a wound which spilled bright red blood between his fingers. With a silly, disconnected grin on his face, he surveyed the room for just a moment, then with effort, walked over to the bar.

"Whiskey," he ordered.

The solemn-faced bartender poured him a glass and Will took it, then turned around to face the silent patrons. By now his side was drenched with blood from his wound, and the blood was beginning to soak into the wide-plank floor.

"Will!" Katie shouted in alarm. She had gone up to her room when he brought her home, and now she hurried back down the stairs and ran over to him.

"Hello, Katie," Will said. He smiled and held his glass out toward her, offering a toast. Then his eyes rolled back in his head and he crumpled to the floor, passed out cold.

Chapter Eleven

"In here," Katie said. "We'll put him in my room."

Gid had been quickly summoned from the restaurant next door, and now he was carrying his brother in his arms. He pushed through the door into Katie's room.

The room was hot and humid, and Katie and Gid could smell the blood from Will's wound. Katie felt around in the dark until she found the bedside table and candle. A moment later she found the box of lucifers and struck one, then held the flame to the candle until a small light perched atop the taper. The dark of the room was pushed away.

"Put him on my bed."

Gid hesitated for a moment. "Do you have any towels or anything to put down? He'll be upset if he finds out he bled on your bed."

"I have an old blanket we can use," Katie offered,

getting one from the bottom draw of the bureau, then spreading it out on her bed.

Gid lay his brother down gingerly. "Did you see who did this to him?"

"No, but some men in the saloon saw them. They said it was a couple of Mexicans from the other side of town," Katie said.

"Why would a couple of Mexicans attack Will?" Gid asked. "We've not done anything to any of them."

"Robbery, perhaps?" Katie suggested.

"Oh, believe me, there are easier ways to make money than tryin' to steal from Will. What about that little pissant Glasscock? Does he know any Mexicans? Maybe he hired 'em."

"That's very possible," Katie said. "There are many Mexicans on the other side of the track who would do anything if the price is right," Katie said. "And I'm sure Mr. Glasscock would be acquainted with such people."

"Yeah, well, if you ask me, Glasscock hired a couple of Mexicans to cut up Will, sure as a gun is iron. Only the Mexicans didn't know what they were gettin' themselves in to, or like as not they wouldn't have done it."

"Two men, attacking him in the dark with knives," Katie said. "He's lucky he wasn't killed."

Gid looked down at his brother. "Yeah, he has bled a lot, hasn't he? You think I should get a doctor?"

Katie shook her head. "There isn't a doctor in San Saba. The nearest one is fifty miles away. But I sometimes help the doctor when he's here, so I know how to treat the wound. Also, I've got some salve, crushed aloe leaves, and plenty of fresh wrappings for bandages. I'd be glad to take care of him."

"I appreciate that," Gid said. "And if you don't mind, I'll just leave him with you until I can get us a room over at the hotel." Gid started to leave, then stopped just before he stepped through the door and looked back toward Katie. "You think I should come back later tonight?"

"No, that won't be necessary," Katie said. "Or even desired. Once I get him bandaged, he'll need to get a good night's sleep." She smiled. "You could probably use a little rest as well. Go on over to the hotel. If I need you, I'll send someone for you, I promise."

"All right, whatever you say," Gid agreed.

When Katie sat on the bed beside Will a few moments later, his eyes snapped open. He saw her reach down to loosen his belt and start unfastening the buttons on his pants.

"What?" Will asked. He tried to sit up. "What are you doing?"

"Shh, lie back down," Katie said quietly. She pushed him back down gently. "I'm trying to help you."

Slowly, Katie began peeling the blood-soaked clothes away from his skin to expose his wound. "I'm going to treat your cut. Then I'm going to wash your clothes."

"You don't have to worry about that. I hate to be a bother. I'll be all right," Will insisted.

"No, you won't be all right unless the wound is cleaned and treated. And you can't walk around wearing blood-soaked clothes," she said. "I have soap and water for your clothes and medicines for you, so I may as well take care of it."

She took off his shirt, then she removed his pants, though for the time being she protected his modesty by the strategic placement of a towel.

Katie sucked in her breath as she looked at the cut, and the blood which had coagulated around the wound. "You've lost quite a bit of blood. It's no wonder you passed out."

"Did I pass out?"

"Yes, of course you did. Do you mean you don't remember?"

"No," Will said. "I remember the fight, and I remember coming into the saloon. Then I don't remember another thing until I woke up just a moment ago."

Katie chuckled. "What do you call that, if it isn't passing out?"

"I guess I would call it going to sleep, real fast," Will

joked. He laughed, then winced as a stab of pain cut through his side.

"You must be still now," Katie instructed. She got up from the bed then walked over to the bureau to pour water from a porcelain pitcher into a basin.

Will lay back and folded his hands behind his head. The muscles in his arms, shoulders, and chest rippled as he did so, and he watched as the beautiful young woman poured the water, then brought it back over to set it on the small bedside table. Again, she sat on the bed beside him.

Gently, she began cleaning the blood from Will's side. The knife wound started just above the belt line, then disappeared below the towel she had put on him. Katie slipped the towel a little farther down. His pubic hair, which began as a tiny dark line at his navel, broadened into a dark, curling bush. As the entire length of the cut was now visible, she stopped before any more of his privacy was compromised.

"It doesn't appear to be too deep," she said as she examined the cut critically. "And I don't think any of your vital organs were cut." She mixed the crushed aloe leaves with the salve and began applying the paste to the wound.

Will took Katie's hand and squeezed it. "You're a fine nurse."

"Unfortunately, I get lots of practice," she said. "The nearest doctor is in Lampasas and that's thirty-five miles away. Doctor Maxwell has taught me a lot."

"This doctor—is he married?"

Katie laughed. "He isn't, but he's close to seventy years old. Why do you ask?"

"I don't know. I was just wondering how it is that a pretty woman like you still lives with her father."

"It hasn't always been like this. I'm a widow," Katie said as she continued to apply the salve. "Isaac Lightburn was a lieutenant in my father's Company. They were both part of General Kirby Smith's Division. Isaac was killed at the Battle of Palmetto Ranch on the Rio Grande."

"Palmetto Ranch? I've heard of that battle. It took place after Lee surrendered at Appomattox. It was even after Jefferson Davis was captured."

"Yes," Katie said. "It was the last battle of the war."

"That was every soldier's worst nightmare, you know," Will said. "To get killed by the last bullet in the last fight of the war."

"And every wife and mother's nightmare as well," Katie said. "My father says that we won that battle. But the fact that we won the battle seemed little consolation when they unloaded Isaac's body from the train. And now, I can't even visit his grave."

"Why not?"

"He was buried in the family cemetery at Brush Creek. Isaac, my mother, my baby sister, my grandparents—

they're all buried on land that now belongs to Hector Laroche, and he won't even let us visit their graves."

"I'm sorry," Will said.

Katie looked at him and smiled wanly. "No, I'm the one who should be sorry," she said. "It was wrong of me to burden you with this, when you have problems of your own." She finished taping the bandage and moved away from the bed.

"I think people need to talk about things like this," Will said. "And if it helped you, I'm glad I was the one you told."

"Does that advice apply to you, too, or do you just try to forget your own past?"

"It's different for a man," Will said and then he paused. "Especially when he's done his fair share of killing."

"Mr. Crockett, are you an outlaw?"

For a long moment, Will stared at her in the lamplight before he spoke, but he felt he should tell her something. He thought about telling her he had ridden with Quantrill, but then he thought of Frank McCain who was lying in the jail awaiting his hanging for the same offence.

Katie Lightburn and her father seemed to be on the good side, but one couldn't be too sure.

"Well, Mr. Crockett, are you an outlaw?" Katie asked again after a protracted silence.

"Some say that I am. Others say that I am a patriot."

"In our own way, the war changed us all." She extinguished the lamp and moved toward the door. "If you need anything, I'll be across the hall."

Will lay in the dark for a long time. He knew Katie—he supposed her name was Lightburn, though she hadn't said as much—was in a bed across the hall. He also knew that there were bargirls who plied their trade in those same rooms.

He hoped Katie wasn't one of them.

Chapter Twelve

When Will awakened the next morning he experienced a moment of confusion as to where he was. But when he moved, a sharp stitch in his side reminded him of what had happened the night before and he reached down to feel the bandage. He was gratified to see that there had been no more bleeding since the previous night.

Will looked around at his surroundings. He knew that he was in Katie's room, but it had been dark when he was brought here, and he hadn't been able to see much.

He didn't know exactly what time it was, but he could tell by the texture of the sunlight streaming in through the window that it was still fairly early in the morning. He also saw his clothes, clean and nearly dry, spread out near the window to take advantage of the warm air and sun.

He lay back in bed for a few more moments, listening to the sounds of a town coming to grips with a new day.

The first sound to get his attention was a heavy, thumping sound. For a moment he didn't recognize it. Then, with a chill, he realized what it had to be. Down at the far end of the street the workers on the hangman's gallows were testing the trapdoor. They were letting it fall open, time and time again. Each successful triggering of the trapdoor was marked with a heavy, rattling thump.

Thump.

Thump.

Thump.

From the blacksmith shop he could hear the sound of the smithy shaping a piece of iron at his forge. The hammer made a ringing sound on the off-beat of the thumping trap door.

Thump.

Ring.

Thump.

Ring.

Thump.

Ring.

Downstairs, the bartender was sweeping off the front porch of the saloon, and he added the scratch of his broom to the thump of the door and the ring of the hammer. Though untended, the result was a rhythmic composition.

Thump, ring, scratch-scratch-scratch ... Thump, ring, scratch-scratch-scratch.

There were other sounds as well: the hollow clop of hooves on the sun baked dirt of the street and the rattle of a freight wagon coming slowly into town. Some children were playing a game of hide-and-seek, and a nearby sign creaked as it moved back and forth in the morning breeze.

The door to his room opened then, and Gid came in, carrying Will's breakfast on a tray.

"How do you feel?" Gid asked.

Will sat up, pleasantly surprised to see that moving wasn't that difficult an ordeal.

"I'm a little sore," he admitted, putting his hand over the bandage to test his wound. "But Katie did a pretty good job of patching me up. I think I'm all right."

"Good. Speaking of Katie, I saw that she was about to bring your breakfast to you, but I told her she didn't have to do that. I figured you'd rather have me bring it."

"Oh, hell yes, of course I'd rather you bring it. I would much rather look at your ugly face than see her again," Will teased as he picked up a piece of bacon from the plate.

"Yeah, well, I had a reason for wanting to see you alone," Gid said.

"It better be a good one." He broke off a piece of biscuit and raked it through the yellow of his fried egg.

Gid held up his finger as if asking Will to wait a minute. Then he stepped to the doorway and looked up and down the hallway to make certain no one was standing just outside, before he closed the door.

"I have something that will definitely interest you," Gid said, "and I don't want to run the risk of anybody overhearing what I have to say."

"Well, what is it?"

"I went by to visit Frank, this morning."

"In jail?"

"Yes."

"Wasn't that a little risky?"

"I told Biddle that I knew some of the men who rode for Quantrill, and I wanted to ask his prisoner about them. Biddle didn't question me at all. In fact, he even left the jail while I was there so Frank and I could talk alone for a few minutes."

"How's Frank holding out?"

"He's pretty nervous about it," Gid said. "He doesn't want to hang."

"Can't say as I blame him. Don't reckon anyone would feel too good in that position."

"Will, do you know why he asked us here?"

"It was supposed to have something to do with money."

"It does have to do with money. Lots of it," Gid replied.

"How much money? And how do we get to it?"

Gid chuckled. "Well, now, that's the problem."

"What do you mean?"

"Frank says he's not goin' to tell us anything more

about it until tomorrow."

"Tomorrow? Hell, what's he talkin' about? There's not goin' to be a tomorrow for Frank. They're plannin' on hangin' him today, aren't they?"

"That's his point, Will. If we want to find out what this is all about, we're goin' to have to get him out of the pickle he's in."

"What did you tell him?"

"I told him don't worry about it, you're a pretty smart fella, you can come up with something," Gid said. He rubbed his hands together and smiled broadly. "So, have you got any ideas?"

"Why do I have to have all the ideas?"

"'Cause you're the smart one. I'm the good-lookin' one," Gid said with a wide grin. "Ma always said so."

"Yeah, well…" Will paused, and looked at his brother, then laughed. "Ma was half right. All right, I'll come up with something. But you're going to have to help me on with my boots," Will said.

"Help you with your boots? Why the hell do I have to help you with your boots?"

Will pushed the rest of his breakfast away. "'Cause we aren't going to be able to stop the hangin' with me layin' in bed."

"All right," Gid said, looking around the room. "I'll help you with your boots."

It was just after noon, and Will and Gid were standing in the alley behind the livery stable.

"Here are the wood shavings you asked for," Gid said, setting a bag down in front of Will. "I got 'em from a pile out behind the cabinet shop."

A couple of horses in the lot whickered, and Will looked around to make certain no one was coming. When he was sure they weren't being watched, he emptied a whole can of kerosene into the sack of wood shavings, then stirred them around so that all of them were wet. After that, he took a piece of rawhide and tied it around the bottom of Gid's right trouser leg so that the cord would hold the pants cuff in a blouse, tight against the boot.

"I still don't know why I'm the one who has to do this," Gid said.

"Because I'm the one who came up with the idea," Will reminded him. "Now, loosen your belt and pull your trouser waist out," Will ordered.

"Just because you—"

Gid's comment was interrupted when Will, suddenly and unceremoniously, dumped the entire sack of shavings down into his pants.

"Hey! What the hell?"

"Push those shavings on down your right pants leg," Will ordered.

"Will, have you gone crazy?"

"You don't want my hand poking around down there, do you, little brother?"

"You stick your hand down there and I'll break it off at the elbow," Gid growled, as he began directing the shavings down his right leg. "These damned things itch," he complained.

"You won't have to put up with them too long," Will promised.

It was about one-thirty when Gid walked, a little stiff-leggedly, down to the gallows. There was still half an hour before the scheduled hanging, but the crowd was already thick, filling the street from porch to porch, jostling for position. Although individually most in the crowd thought that the hanging was an unjust penalty for someone who had done nothing more than ride with Quantrill during the war, there was nevertheless, a festive air to the crowd. The celebration came from the fact that a hanging was a spectator event of the first order.

The crowd was made up of a cross section of the town. Standing unobtrusively at the rear of the crowd were a score or more of Mexican men, wearing peasant shirts, colorful serapes, and wide, fringe-brimmed sombreros.

Nearby, an old Mexican woman was selling tortillas from a box she carried. She didn't have any teeth, and she kept her mouth closed so tightly that her chin and nose nearly touched. A swarm of flies buzzed around the box, drawn by the pungent aromas of beans and sauces. She worked with quick, deft fingers, rolling the spicy ingredients into tortillas, then handing them to her customers.

The Americans, many of whom were the old woman's customers, were variously dressed in suits, shirtsleeves, and overalls; the women wore long dresses and bonnets and watched over the children, who threaded in and out of the groups as they chased one another, laughing at their games.

To one side of the crowd, on the opposite side of the street from the jail, a black-frocked preacher stood on an overturned box, taking advantage of the gathering to deliver a fiery sermon. The man was of average height and build, with a full head of thick black hair. Standing on the box, he jabbed his finger repeatedly toward the gallows as he harangued the crowd.

"In a few moments, a poor miserable sinner is going to be hurled to eternity… sent to meet his Maker with blood on his hands and sin in his heart."

Several of the Mexicans, upon hearing that, crossed themselves and mouthed a quick prayer.

"No such thing, Preacher! That fella rode with Quantrill and he didn't do nothin' more'n kill a few Yankees!" someone shouted.

"He didn't kill enough of 'em, is my way of thinkin'," another added, and the crowd laughed and cheered the hecklers.

"Hell, yes! Instead of hangin' him, we ought to elect him to Congress!"

"Congress wouldn't take 'im! He ain't a big enough sinner!"

There was more laughter.

Undaunted, the preacher continued his sermon. He waggled his finger at the crowd. "Brothers and sisters, hear this now! That sinner is goin' to be cast into Hell because he has not repented of his sins!"

"Good for him!"

"Tell him to give the Devil a kick in the ass from me!"

There was more nervous laughter.

"It's too late for him, brothers and sisters. It's too late to save his soul, and he is consigned to the fiery furnace of Hell, doomed to writhe in agony forever!"

Again, the Mexicans crossed themselves, and now, even among the Americans in the crowd, the preacher's words began to sink in. A few shivered involuntarily at the powerful imagery of burning forever. One or two of them touched their necks fearfully, and a few souls, perhaps weak on willpower, sneaked a drink from a bottle.

"It's too late for him, but it's not too late for you! Repent! Repent now, I say, for the wages of sin are death and eternal damnation!"

Gid moved quietly and unobserved through the crowd. The preacher had everyone's attention, which was exactly what he needed. With a lit cigar in his mouth, he moved over to stand directly adjacent to the foot of the gallows, where a pile of sawdust and wood shavings remained from the recent construction.

Gid reached down with his knife and cut the rawhide cord that had bloused his trouser leg. Then he shook the pants leg to allow the coal-oil-soaked shavings to fall out of the bottom of his pants. That done, he took several more puffs on the cigar to get the tip glowing brightly, then dropped the cigar in the pile of shavings.

It took but a moment for the shavings to flame up. As soon as Gid saw that the fire had caught, he moved back into the crowd, edging over to the opening between the jailhouse and the hardware store.

"After this, here hangin' takes place," the preacher was saying, "I invite all of you to come down to the creek with me! Come down to the creek and get right with God! Ask Him to save your souls from eternal perdition and I will dunk you in His cleansing waters. I will ... *oh shit!*" the preacher suddenly shouted.

"What'd you say preacher?" somebody in the crowd asked, shocked by the preacher's outburst.

"Fire!" the preacher shouted, pointing to the gallows.

"The damned gallows is on fire!"

The crowd turned to see what the preacher was talking about, and they saw flames shooting up the side of the gallows, licking over onto the gallows floor, and leaping up to the cross-beam where the rope, already in place, was also burning.

The women screamed and the men swore. Sheriff Martin and his deputies, the hangman, and Constable Biddle all ran out of the jailhouse to see what was going on.

"Damn! How did this happen? Buckets! Get the buckets!" Martin shouted in agitation.

Mothers began calling for their children as several men ran to get buckets to extinguish the flames. In all the confusion, no one saw Gid moving quickly through the narrow passageway between the jail and the hardware store.

In the alley behind the hardware store, three saddled horses were tied. Gid untied them, mounted one, then held the reins of the other two, keeping them ready.

Sixty feet away Will started running back toward the horses. Behind Will, against the back wall of the jail, a little string of smoke began working up from a sputtering fuse. The fuse was attached to a keg of gunpowder.

There was a brilliant flash of light, then a loud blast as the planted bomb exploded. The back wall of the jail came crashing down into the alley, and a moment later, a short, bandy-legged man, coughing and waving at the acrid gun smoke, picked his way through the rubble.

"Are you all right, Frank?" Will shouted.

"Yeah!" Frank answered, still waving at the smoke and the powdered brick hanging in the air as a result of the pulverized wall. The dust from the explosion had peppered his beard, making it look white.

Will and Gid rode up to him, leading the third horse. Frank swung into the saddle. Then the three horses bolted into a gallop as if they were shot from a cannon. So complete was the surprise, that no one even saw them leave.

Chapter Thirteen

Will, Gid, and Frank were at the Pauley way station, a gray, weather-beaten building which sat baking in the afternoon sun. A faded sign just outside the door of the building gave the arrival and departure schedule of stagecoaches that no longer ran, for a line that no longer existed. The stage line had been abandoned three years earlier when the railroad reached Brownwood from Lampasas.

The roof and one wall of the nearby barn were caved in, but there was an overhang at the other end that provided some much-needed shade for their horses. Frank was sitting on the front porch with his back against the wall. Will was inside the building, looking around at what remained of a once-busy passenger terminal.

Gid was outside, by the pump. A little earlier, he had taken the pump apart, and now he was reassembling it.

Will stepped back out onto the front porch.

"Find anything interesting in there, Will?" Gid asked from his position, bent over the pump.

"Not really," Will answered. He looked down at Frank. "All right, Frank, we've done our part. We came to San Saba like you wanted. We even busted you out of jail. Now it's time for you to tell us what this is all about."

"I've told you all I know," Frank replied.

"Tell us again."

"I met a fella some weeks back in a saloon back in Henderson. He said his name was Tim Wilson. We got to talkin' some 'bout what we done durin' the war, and turns out our paths musta crossed, only we just never know'd it. I mean, me an' him had never run acrost each other before, but he know'd lots of the same folks we know'd. Like ole' Bill Anderson, and George Todd. Hell, he even know'd Quantrill."

"They're all dead," Will said.

"I know they're dead. What's that got to do with anything?"

"It means we have no way of checking him out."

"He's all right," Frank said.

"How do you know?"

"I can feel it."

"That's it? You feel it?"

"Will," Gid said, looking up from the pump. "We went by Frank's feelin's a lot durin' the war, and he never

127

steered us wrong."

"Yeah," Frank said. "Why you doubtin' me now?"

Will paused for a minute, then nodded. "Gid's right," he said. "All right, Frank, if you think this Tim Wilson is tellin' you straight, then that's good enough for me. Now, tell us the rest again."

"After he found out I once rode with Quantrill, he asked me could I round up any of the other fellas who was still around. So I asked him, what for?

"'I've got a little job in mind,' he says.

"'What kind of job?' I asks.

"'One that'll let you and the fellas you round up make a lot of money,' he says.

"'I'm always lookin' for some easy money,' I says.

"'This ain't exactly takin' candy off a babe. You goin' to have to take some risks,' he says.

"'What kind of risks?' I asks.

"'Same kind of risks you took when you was ridin' with Quantrill,' he says. Only this time, you'll get to keep a lot more of what you take.'"

"But he didn't say how much?" Will asked.

Frank shook his head. "He just said there was a lot of it. More'n any of us had ever seen before."

"What do you think, Will?" Gid asked.

"It depends on what money we're talking about. If it's money that belongs to decent, hardworking people, I don't want anything to do with it."

Frank chuckled. "Believe me, there ain't nothin' innocent about the people that has this money."

"All right, I'm in. But, I think if there's a lot of money, we'd better be getting an equal share," Will replied. "If we share equally in the risk, then we are going to share equally in the money."

"He didn't say nothin' 'bout whether the share would be equal or not. He just said there'd be lots of money," Frank said.

"Equal," Will said again.

"What if he won't go along with that?" Frank asked. "I mean, it's his plan. He may figure he deserves more. And I don't want to pass up the deal, not if it means a lot of money."

Will smiled. "My reckoning is that he'll go along with it. He really has no choice. He can't do it alone, or he wouldn't have asked us in on the job. And it's too late for him to get anyone else."

"Yeah, you may have a point," Frank agreed.

"Hey," Gid called, smiling broadly as he began working the pump handle up and down. "Hey, you fellas, look at this! It's moving real smooth now! I think I fixed it."

"Don't do no good to have a working pump if there ain't no water down there," Frank said.

"There's water down there," Gid answered. He started

toward the barn.

"Where you goin'?" Frank asked.

"To the horses. I'm going to get my canteen so I can prime the pump."

"Gid, wait a minute! Do you think that's a good idea?" Will asked. "If you use up all your water trying to prime this pump, there's no telling where we're going to find some more."

"There's water down there, Will, I can smell it. Only we aren't going to get it if the pump's not primed."

"You use all your water up, don't think you're goin' to get any of mine," Frank warned him.

"Hell, as I recall, it's not your water anyway," Gid called back. "I seem to mind that you were in jail. We had to dig up a horse and tack for you."

Gid returned a moment later with his canteen. He unscrewed the cap and held it over the pump for a second, then, with a shrug of resignation, poured it in. The water glistened brightly in the sun, then gurgled as it all rushed down the pipe.

Gid began working the handle. "It's comin'!" he said. "I can feel it!"

Will moved over to the pump, and even Frank stood up to watch.

Suddenly the suction was broken, and the pump handle began to move easily again.

"Damn!" Gid said. "I lost it."

"Tole' you," Frank said, moving back over to resume his position on the porch.

"Will, let me have your water."

"Gid..."

"Come on, Will, it was almost there. I could feel it. Think about it. Wouldn't some cool deep-well water taste good about now? And there would also be plenty of water for the horses. And a bath! Will, hell, we could even take us a bath!"

"A bath?" Frank said. "Why the hell would you want to take a bath? Out here, you'll just get dirty again."

"You sure there's water down there, Gid?" Will asked.

"I'm tellin' you, Will, it was right there. I just lost the suction, that's all."

"All right," Will finally agreed. "I'll get my canteen."

Frank sat back down on the edge of the porch, reached down to pull up a straw, then stuck the end of it in his mouth. "You two boys is crazy, you know that?" he asked. "You're throwin' away good drinkin' water on the chance there might be some in that well. And for what reason? So's you can take a bath."

Will came back a moment later, carrying a canteen. He handed it to Gid, who then poured it into the top of the pump. Once again, Gid began pumping.

"Yes!" he said, after a moment. "Yes, it's coming!"

Will stood by watching with intense interest, and again Frank came over to see what was happening.

"Shit!" Gid shouted. "Shit, I need some more water to hold the suction. It's almost there, but I may lose it. I need more water!"

"Well, don't look at me," Frank said. "You ain't gettin' my water."

"We already got your water," Will replied. "That was your canteen I just got."

"What?"

Will started toward the horses again. "Don't lose the suction, Gid. I'll get my canteen."

"Hurry!" Gid called.

Will ran to his horse, got his canteen, then ran back.

"Pour it in while I'm still pumpin'," Gid said.

"You crazy sonsofbitches!" Frank shouted. "You've used up ever' damn bit of our water!"

Ignoring him, Will began to pour as Gid continued to pump.

There were more gurgling sounds as the water disappeared down the pipe. For several long, anxious seconds, Will and Frank watched as Gid continued to pump, the only sound being the squeak and clank of the pump handle and piston.

Suddenly a big smile spread across Gid's face. "Get ready," he said. "Here it comes!"

At that moment, water began pouring out of the mouth of the pump. For the first few seconds, the water was red with rust. Then it cleared.

"Look at that!" Gid said. "Isn't it beautiful the way it's flashin' and sparkling like that? Why, it looks like I'm pumpin' pure sunlight!"

Will cupped his hands under the cascading water, then bent down to take a drink.

"How is it?" Frank asked anxiously. "How does it taste?"

Will took several, deep swallows, then stood up with water running down his chin.

"Oh, that's fine!" he said. "Gid, you remember when we were with Quantrill and we hit Shawnee Station?"

"Yes."

"We got some champagne there, remember?"

Gid smiled. "Yeah, I remember. We got two cases of it."

Will pointed to the water that was still cascading down from the pump. By now the water splashing on the ground was beginning to form little rivulets.

"Well, little brother, that champagne wasn't half as good-tasting as this."

"Yahoo!" Gid said. "Here, you pump! Let me have a drink!"

Will took over the pump while first Gid and then Frank drank their fill. Next they filled their canteens. Then they found a bucket and took water to the watering trough for their horses.

Finally, they dragged another trough over to the pump so they could pump water directly into it. When it was full, they stepped back to look at what they had done. Ten thousand points of light danced on the undulating surface.

"There you go, big brother. It's ready for your bath."

"No," Will said. "It was your idea, and you're the one who fixed the pump. You go first."

Gid smiled broadly, then began stripping out of his clothes.

Gid had finished his bath, and Will, with his cigar tilted at a jaunty angle, was sitting in the tub toward the end of his own bath, when the three riders arrived.

"Here they come," Frank said, shielding his eyes. "The fella on the right is Tim. Don't know the other two."

Gid came around to stand with Frank as they waited for the riders. Will didn't get out of the water.

"Wasn't sure you would be here," Tim said to Frank. "Word I got was that you got yourself throwed in jail and was goin' to get hung."

"I was in jail," Frank replied. He smiled. "But my two pards here busted me out."

"These the boys you was talkin' about? The Crocketts?" Tim dismounted and walked over to the water trough, then splashed some water on his face. "Damn, where'd this water come from?"

"Gid fixed the pump," Frank said. "This is Gid." Frank indicated the man standing beside him. The one takin' the bath is Will."

Tim was lanky and rawboned, with a handlebar moustache. One of the two riders with him was a big man, almost as large as Gid, though he was perhaps twenty years older, with salt-and-pepper hair and beard. The third rider was small and clean-shaven. This rider seemed to be eyeing Will with a bemused expression.

"You goin' to introduce these two?" Gid asked,

Drying his face with his bandanna, Tim nodded toward the riders who had come in with him, neither of whom had yet dismounted.

"The big fella there is John Cook. He was a colonel with General Jo Shelby."

"Colonel Cook, I've heard of you, sir," Will said.

"And I have heard of you, Mister Crockett," Cook replied.

"And this is—," Tim said, but he was interrupted by Will standing up in the water. As the water only came to a little above his knees, his nudity was completely exposed.

"Mister, I see you've been eyein' the bathwater," Will said easily. "I'm finished now, you're welcome to it if you'd like a bath."

"Anita Sheldon," Tim finished.

Anita took off her hat and shook her head, allowing long tresses of fire-red hair to cascade down around her shoulders.

Seeing that it was a woman, Will sat down again, so quickly that he splashed water everywhere. Anita laughed.

"Damn it, Tim, you could'a said somethin' sooner," Will said.

"Why, Mr. Crockett," Anita said in a soft, husky voice. "It doesn't say much for me that you can't tell I'm a woman just by looking."

"Well, you had your hat pulled so low, and those pants and that shirt," Will sputtered.

Anita laughed again. "You don't have to explain," she said. "I dressed this way purposely. Until this is all over with, I'm going to have to pass as a man."

"Yes, well, you *ain't* a man," Will said. He held out his hand and moved it in a small circle. "So if you would, please, just turn around until I get out of here and get dressed."

"Really, Mr. Crockett, I've already seen you. What is there to hide, now?" Anita continued to appraise him with her cool, green eyes. Her lips were curled in the suggestion of a smile, which accented her high cheekbones.

As Will studied her, he began to wonder how he could have mistaken her for a man. He could see now that she was really quite a pretty woman.

"I reckon you're right at that," he said, standing up again.

Anita had actually been teasing him, and had no idea he would call her bluff. When he stood up to expose himself again, she was caught off guard, and she cleared her throat in embarrassment.

"Perhaps I *should* give you a little privacy," she said, turning her horse around.

"By the way, Miss Sheldon," Will said as he began drying off. "My offer still goes. If you want to take a bath, you're welcome to jump in the water."

"Thank you, Mr. Crockett," Anita replied. "You will understand, I'm sure, if I decline your generous proposition."

"If you folks will climb down, I'll take your horses," Frank offered. "There's water and shade for 'em over to the barn."

"Thank you," Cook said as he dismounted. By now, Will had pulled on his trousers and Cook looked back toward Anita. "You can turn around now, my dear," he said. "Mr. Crockett is decent."

"Thank you," Anita said. She too dismounted, and handed the reins of her horse to Frank.

Will began to rewrap the bandage around his waist.

"Oh, you are wounded!" Anita said.

"Yeah, I had a run-in with a couple of Mexicans."

"It looks very recent," Anita said. "When did it

happen?"

"About four days ago," Will answered.

"Mr. Wilson," Cook said. "I told you to get responsible men, not men who are likely to get into bar fights."

"You said get someone like Quantrill's Raiders," Tim replied. "Well these, here fellas ain't *like* Quantrill's Raiders, they *are* Quantrill's Raiders. And that means they ain't Sunday School teachers."

"It wasn't a bar fight, Colonel Cook," Gid explained. "And my brother didn't start it. But if you don't want us in on this, just let us know and we'll be going on our way."

"No, no," Cook said, holding up his hand. "I'm sorry if I seemed judgmental. It's just that in order for this to work, we are going to have to have as much self-discipline as we do skill and daring."

"We can be as disciplined as we need to be," Will said. "For our fair share," he added. He dropped one end of the bandage and had to start reapplying it.

"Here, you'd better let me help," Anita suggested, stepping over to take the bandage wrapping from him.

"Thanks."

Anita started wrapping the bandage around him, carefully and skillfully. When her fingers touched his skin they managed to be hot and cool at the same time.

"You do this well," Will said.

"I have a knack for it," Anita said.

"Colonel, you want to tell us what this is all about?" Will asked, looking up at Cook.

"All right," Cook answered. "But first, I think I need to tell you a little about General Jo Shelby. You men knew him, of course?"

"Commanding general of the Missouri Cavalry," Gid said. "Of course we knew him."

"What you may not know is that, after the surrender, General Shelby decided to keep his men together. We left Missouri and marched through Arkansas and Texas, all the way to the Rio Grande, where, rather than surrender our flag, we buried it in the river."

"I heard you all had done something like that," Will said. Anita was finished with the bandaging, and he began putting on his shirt.

"Something happened during that last mission that has a bearing on what we are about," Cook continued. "As we passed through Austin we learned that a group of brigands and deserters had taken it upon themselves to loot the state treasury. And although it wasn't our state, it wasn't our money, and it wasn't even our cause, General Shelby decided that our honor lay in dispersing the robbers and saving the money for the people of Texas."

"You did that?" Gid asked.

"We did that, yes. We killed nearly all of the robbers and returned the money."

"You had your hands on all that money and you returned it?" Frank asked. He shook his head. "General Shelby must've had a great deal of control over his men to convince them to do that."

"If you remember General Shelby, you know that is so," Cook said. "But I must tell you, if we had known then what we know now, I don't believe even General Shelby would have returned that money to the vault."

"Why do you say that?"

"Less than one week after we passed through Austin, the Union Army arrived to begin their occupation duty. The first thing they did was take the money from the vault and transfer it to the Federal Treasury."

"Hell, what did you expect, Colonel? The Yankees won," Will said.

"I could accept that if all the money they took had made it to the Federal Treasury," Cook said. "But less than one half of the money reached the Federal Government. The commanding general of the Tenth Kansas Cavalry Brigade siphoned off the rest of it. He then resigned from the army, and has subsequently used that money to bribe tax collectors and buy himself a sheriff. He now owns much of the land and most of the businesses in the towns. He's turned San Saba County into his own little kingdom."

"You must be talking about Hector Laroche," Will said.

"Yes," Cook said. "You've met him?"

Will shook his head. "I haven't met him, but I've heard all about him. And I have a particular interest in one of his hirelings."

"Ah, you would be talking about his sheriff, Felix Martin," Cook said. "Perhaps you ran across him before? He was a first sergeant in Otto Hoffman's company of Jayhawkers. Hoffman's Jayhawkers, of course, being a part of Laroche's Tenth Kansas Cavalry Brigade."

"Oh, yes, I know about him," Will said.

"I'm not sure, but I believe Hoffman got himself killed."

"He did get himself killed," Will said.

"You say that with a sense of absolute certainty."

"Yeah, well I can be certain, because I'm the one that killed him."

"I don't hear any sense of regret in your statement."

"That's because I have no sense of regret. Colonel, if ever there was a man who needed killin', it was Otto Hoffman," Gid said.

"Believe me, I'm not finding fault with his being killed," Cook said. "I've heard stories of how he raided farms and killed innocent people. They say he and his men sometimes raped the women."

"Let's change the subject," Will suggested.

"Of course," Cook said.

"There's another fella I met in San Saba," Will said.

"An ornery young cuss named Lee Glasscock. Do either of you know anything about him?"

"I know quite a bit about him, Mr. Crockett," Anita said, speaking up then. "He is my brother."

"Your brother?"

"My half-brother, to be more accurate," Anita said. "We had the same mother, but different fathers. When Lee's father died, my mother married my father. Lee's father was from Kansas, my father was from Texas. When the war began, my father returned to Texas and my mother and I came with him. Lee stayed in Kansas with an aunt and uncle on his father's side."

"I'm sure you must've asked yourself why we would have a woman involved with this job," Cook said, then. "Perhaps it will help you to understand when I tell you that the uncle Lee Glasscock stayed with is General Hector Laroche."

"What does that have to do with Miss Sheldon?" Will asked. "She just explained that Hector Laroche is Glasscock's uncle, not hers."

Anita dipped her handkerchief into the water and wrung it out.

"Hector Laroche may be my brother's uncle," she said, as she began patting her face with the wet cloth.

She aimed a penetrating stare toward Will.

"But he is my lover."

Chapter Fourteen

It was dark.

Will was sitting on the edge of the porch, eating peaches from a can. The meadow between the building and the tree line glowed in a soft luminescent yellow from the winking of hundreds of fireflies. High overhead, the black-velvet sky was filled with stars which ranged in magnitude from pulsating white all the way down to a barely perceptible blue dust.

Will had taken his supper with the others inside the building but he came outside to eat his peaches and get a breath of fresh air. Colonel Cook had not yet filled them in on what he had in mind, though he'd promised to do that before everyone bedded down for the night.

Will heard someone walking across the porch behind him. Without turning around, he spoke.

"Evenin', Miss Sheldon."

"That's very good," Anita said. "How did you know it was me?"

"Your steps are lighter and quicker than the others," Will said. He held out his can. "Would you like the rest of my peaches?"

"Why, how nice of you to share," Anita replied, sitting on the porch beside him.

"I have sort of a weakness for canned peaches," Will admitted. "I almost always have three or four cans in my saddlebags." He chuckled. "I'm not sure my horse appreciates my habit."

Anita took Will's spoon and began eating.

"They are very good," she said as she took the first bite.

"Miss Sheldon, may I ask you a question?"

"It's Will, isn't it? Don't you think you could call me Anita now? I mean, we're going to be working together."

"All right, Anita, but that's my question. If your brother is Laroche's nephew, and if you are his woman..."

"I am *not* his woman," Anita said quickly, interrupting Will in mid-sentence.

"I thought you said..."

"I said he was my lover," she corrected. "There is a difference. I have no more feeling for him than a whore does for the men who visit her."

"Then why?"

"I do it for the same reasons the whores do it," Anita

144

said. "Only, I will be getting a lot more money than any whore has ever gotten."

"Then it is just the money?"

"Yes," she answered quickly. Then, after a pause, she said, "No. It's not just the money."

"What else?"

"I told you that when the war started my father moved us to Texas. When he got here, he joined the Confederate army. During the war he led a patrol into Kansas. He was caught, and even though he was in uniform when he was caught, he wasn't treated as a prisoner of war. Instead he was tried as a spy, and he was hanged."

"I'm sorry to hear that," Will said.

"General Laroche could have interceded on my father's behalf. My mother wrote to him, begging that he do so, but she got no answer from him. After the war, when he came to Texas, he told my mother and me that he never received the letter, and that he didn't know about my father until it was too late.

"We believed him. Then his wife died and he offered me a job managing his household. It seemed like a respectable enough position, with good pay, so I accepted.

"But one day, when I was looking for something, I happened to find in his papers my mother's letter to him. I also found a letter from General Halleck suggesting leniency for my father. Most damning of all was General

Laroche's answer to General Halleck. 'As the Federal Government has not recognized the Confederacy as a legitimate government, then it follows that their army is not a legitimate army,' he said in his letter. 'Therefore I believe the sentence of death I have imposed upon Major Sheldon to be correct.'" She sighed. "I think it was the fact that he lied to us that disturbed me more than anything else. He swore to us that he did not know about my father until it was too late, when in fact, he was the one who ordered my father's execution."

They were silent for another moment. Then Anita continued. "That was when I decided I would kill him."

"I reckon I can understand you wantin' to kill him, all right," Will said. "But sleepin' with him seems to me to be a funny way of doin' it."

"Perhaps not," Anita replied with a wry smile. "Do you know why the black widow spider is called a black widow?"

"No, I can't say as I do."

"It is because after she mates with the male spider, she kills him."

"Damn," Will said. "I'm glad I'm not a male spider." He looked at her and smiled. "Although I guess if I got randy enough, I might be willin' to take the chance. Especially if it was with someone who looked like you."

Anita smiled at his comment, then continued with

her explanation. "I figured letting Laroche into my bed would allow me to gain his confidence, which would make things easier. I started out thinking I wanted to kill him, but when I found out just how much money he has managed to steal since coming to Texas, I came up with another idea. Losing all of his money would be worse than death to him. And it would be much more profitable for me."

"And that's about the time Colonel Cook got in touch with you?"

"Not quite," Anita said. "Colonel Cook didn't recruit me. I recruited him."

"You mean...this is all *your* idea?

"Every bit of it," Anita replied.

At that moment, Cook stuck his head through the door.

"Anita, my dear, Mr. Crockett, would you two like to come inside. I think it's time we went over the plans."

Will stood up and brushed off the seat of his pants. "Yes, indeed, I'm ready," he said. "I don't want to miss this." He held out his hand to help Anita to her feet.

Inside, on what had been the ticket counter, Cook spread out a large hand-drawn map. He kept the corners from rolling back up by the application of four disparate weights: a rock, a pistol, a can of beans, and a coffee pot.

"Gather around the map now," Cook said.

The map showed a stretch of railroad, with all the adjacent terrain features clearly marked.

"Next Wednesday a two-car train will make a run from San Saba to Lampasas," Cook said. "One car will be General Laroche's private car. The other will be an express car. Gentlemen, this is no ordinary express car." Cook pointed to the lower right-hand side of the paper, to the drawing of a railroad car.

"The walls of this car are reinforced with steel, so that they are bullet-proof. It is also fitted front and rear on both sides with firing slots. But what makes it most dangerous is this." Cook tapped the end of his pencil on something that stuck up from the top.

"What is that? A smokestack?" Tim asked.

"It's a turret," Cook explained.

"A turret?" Gid asked. "What's a turret?"

"It's a cylinder with a gun attached, fitted so it can turn three hundred and sixty degrees. It's not an original idea. I'm afraid the designer of this car borrowed the concept from Mr. Ericson's ironclad ship, the *Monitor*. This ability to turn means that one man, protected by the steel sides of the turret, can spin all the way around to face a threat, no matter from which direction it may be posed."

"I'll be damned," Frank said.

"And there is something else," Cook added. Again, he

148

touched the turret with the end of his pencil. "The gun that will be firing through the firing slit on this turret is probably unlike any gun any of you have ever seen before. It is capable of extremely rapid fire."

"That would be a Gatling gun?" Will asked.

Cook looked up in surprise. "Yes. Are you familiar with the Gatling gun?"

"I've never seen one, but I've heard of them," Will said. "They're guns with several barrels and you turn a crank to make them all fire fast."

"Yes. That crank not only rotates the barrels, it also ejects the old cartridge and loads new ones," Cook said.

"Lordy, wouldn't I love to see that, though?" Gid said.

"I'm afraid you will see it, Mr. Crockett," Cook said. "Unfortunately, you will see it from the wrong side."

"Colonel, you've made your point as to how difficult it is going to be to stop this train," Will said. "Now, tell us why we *should* stop it."

"Why, to get at the money the express car is carrying, of course."

"That's my next question. How much money is in there?"

Cook smiled. "I know that some of you have been wondering just what Miss Sheldon's role is in all this. I'm going to let her answer the question as to just how much money we're talking about."

"The amount of money the express car will be carrying

that day is three hundred thousand dollars," Anita said.

"Whew!" Frank said, whistling.

"That's fifty thousand dollars each," Will said quickly.

"Not quite," Cook said. "Not all shares will be equal."

"Colonel, you just described a train car that is built like the *Monitor*, and you expect us to go up against it. We'll do it, and we'll get the money it's carrying. But we're going to divide it equally."

"I'm afraid you don't understand," Cook started, but Anita cut him off with a raised hand.

"There are some others involved," Anita said. "Their cut is ten thousand."

"Will the others be taking the same risks?" Will asked.

"No," Anita said. "But they are necessary."

Tim and Gid looked at Will. He ran his hand through his hair, then nodded.

"All right," Will finally said. "I reckon I can go along with that."

"Good," Anita said, obviously relieved that there wouldn't be a problem. "Colonel, you want to go on with your plan?"

"Very well," Cook said. He pointed to the express car again. "As long as this Gatling gun is operating, one man can hold off an entire troop of cavalry. So, the first thing we have to do is get rid of the turret."

"Any ideas?" Frank asked.

Cook shook his head. "All I've come up with, so far, is *what* has to be done. Just *how* it is to be done is yet to be worked out," he answered.

"All right, what else has to be done?" Will asked.

"The train has to be stopped. The guards in the express car have to be taken care of. The doors to the car have to be breached, and once we are inside, the vault has to be opened."

"It's easy enough to stop the train," Gid said. "All we have to do is pull up some of the track."

"That won't work," Anita said.

"Why not?"

"Laroche is no fool. He knows that this train is going to make an attractive target, so he is sending a pilot engine and a track repair crew half an hour ahead," she explained.

"And, even if we got it stopped, there is still the problem of the express car and the Gatling gun," Cook said.

What if we buried a bomb under the track?" Will suggested. "We could set it off just as the train arrives."

"That could get some innocent people killed," Anita said.

"Who on board that train is innocent?"

"The engineer and fireman," Anita suggested. "They are both men with families just trying to earn a living. And then, of course, there is me." She smiled. "Although

I'd be the first to admit that calling me innocent begs the term."

"Wait a minute. *You're* going to be on that train?"

"She has to be," Cook said.

"Why is that?"

"Because once you do get the train stopped and get into the express car, I am the only one who can open the vault for you." She smiled. "I know the combination."

"There you have it, gentlemen, all the details," Colonel Cook said. "Surely, if we all put our heads together, we will come up with a workable plan."

Chapter Fifteen

Although everyone had thrown their bedrolls down inside, Will woke in the middle of the night feeling hot and stuffy. Thinking it would be cooler outside, he got up a little after midnight, gathered his bedroll, then picked his way quietly through the snoring, sleeping bodies.

He spread his blankets out on a small, grassy knoll about fifteen yards from the building and lay down. The stars were so clear and bright that he almost felt as if he could reach up and pluck one from the night sky. He saw a falling star, and he spent a moment wondering what caused them to sometimes become dislodged.

A creaking sound on the front porch caused him to grab his pistol and raise up quickly. He looked toward the source of the sound, then saw that someone else was abandoning the building. At first, whoever it was was hidden in the shadows of the porch. Then the person walked over to the pump and into a silver splash of moonlight.

It was Anita.

Will called out to her.

"Oh!" she said. "I thought I was alone."

"Couldn't sleep?"

"I got too hot."

"Yeah, I did too."

They were silent for a moment.

"Will, what is it like?"

Will was confused by her question. "What is what like?"

"To live the life of an outlaw? To be as free as a bird, to go where you want, when you want, and to be beholden to nobody?"

"That sounds good to you, does it?"

"Yes."

"I didn't plan this life, Anita." Will pulled up a stem of grass, then began sucking on the cool, sweet root.

"What kind of life did you plan?"

"I figured I'd be a farmer, marry some girl from a neighboring farm, or maybe from town. By all rights I should be raising a couple of kids about now, worrying about rain and helping my neighbors put up a barn or a granary."

Anita laughed softly. "It's hard to imagine you as a farmer, Will Crockett."

Will laughed with her. "Yeah," he said. "Well, to tell

you the truth, my pa shared your opinion. 'You was born to hang,' he used to say."

"I guess the war changed the plans of a lot of people," Anita said.

"I reckon so."

"What are you going to do with your money?"

"Nothing."

"Nothing?"

"I've got this funny habit," Will said.

"What's that?"

"I don't spend money until I actually have it in my hands."

"Don't you even like to think about it?"

"No."

"Well, I know what I'm going to do," she said. "I'm going to San Fran—" she stopped. "Come to think of it, maybe it would be better if I were more like you. There's no sense in my spending money I don't have."

"Money doesn't mean anything anyway," Will said.

"How can you say that?"

"If you've got enough money for a good horse and saddle, enough to keep a few necessary items in your saddlebags..."

"Like canned peaches?" Anita interrupted.

"Like canned peaches," Will agreed with a little chuckle. "Plus a few coins to buy yourself a steak dinner, have a few drinks, play some cards, what need is there for more money?"

"Well, I do have a few more wants than that." Anita yawned. "Right now, I'd like to get a little sleep."

Will patted the ground beside him. "Well, you could spread your blankets here, beside me."

Anita chuckled. "I believe I said I would like to get a little *sleep*," she said pointedly.

As Will lay on his blanket awaiting sleep, he listened to the rhythmic breathing of the young woman who was lying beside him. The more he was around her, the more he wondered how he could have possibly mistaken her for a man when he first saw her.

Anita was a very attractive woman, more than that, there was a great sensuality to her, and though sensual wasn't a word with which Will was familiar, he was certainly aware of the condition.

Anita had said that she was sharing the bed of General Laroche, doing so not out of any attraction to him, but to take advantage of him. Will couldn't help to be aroused by his proximity to her, and by the candid discussion of her sex life.

He was certain that if he approached her now that she would be receptive, not only that, she may have come out here to join him tonight for that very reason. He fought back the urge however, believing that any such entanglement would cause complications. And the success of the mission before them could well be hampered by those complications.

It was difficult to put her out of his mind but he had the strength of will to do just that. Finally, he was able to go to sleep.

"Damn, big brother, you planning on sleeping your life away?" Gid asked.

Will opened his eyes and saw Gid squatting on his haunches, looking over at him. Gid was holding two steaming cups of coffee, and he handed one cup to Will.

"Thanks," Will said, sitting up. He looked around and saw that several of the others were up. But he didn't see Cook or Anita.

"Cook and Miss Sheldon still asleep?" he asked.

"Asleep? Hell no," Gid answered. "They got up and left before the sun came up."

"I'll be damned," Will said.

"Come on inside," Gid invited. "You've got some plannin' to do."

"*I've* got some planning to do?" Will asked as he pulled on his boots. "What do you mean *I've* got some planning to do?"

"How we're going to get the train stopped and get into

the express car," Gid answered. "I told the others you were really good at figuring out stuff like that."

"Oh, you did, did you?"

"Yep," Gid said, smiling broadly. "So they decided to put you in charge."

"Put me in charge? I thought Colonel Cook was in charge."

"Ah, you know how colonels are," Gid said. "They're big ones for tellin' you what do to, then sittin' back an' lettin' you do it. When it comes time to hit the train, it'll be just us. And I'd feel a heap better about you leadin' us than I would if it was Tim or Frank."

Chapter Sixteen

Hector Laroche was a very large man. The men who worked for him were fond of saying that he would "dress out" at over 300 pounds. Rather than try to hide his weight, he played it up, wearing ruffled shirts and a gold watch chain which stretched across his vest. He didn't wear a beard, but had bushy muttonchop sideburns framing jowls which hung like saddlebags from each side of his face. He had no visible neck. Instead, a series of chins started somewhere just under his rubbery lips, then trailed down to the top of his chest.

Laroche was sitting at a large, polished mahogany table in his dining room, and he reached for a little silver bell, then picked it up and shook it. The melodic dinging brought a young, attractive Mexican woman out of the kitchen.

"*Si*, Señor General?" she asked.

"Maria, I would like you to bring me some more pancakes," Laroche said.

"*Si*, Señor General."

"Oh, and Maria?" Laroche called as she started toward the kitchen. Maria stopped. "Only about nine or ten this time," he said. "I'm just about full."

"*Si*, Señor General."

When Maria left, Laroche looked toward the opposite end of the table. This morning he had ordered Maria to set a place for Anita, but she had not yet returned. He was a little irritated by her absence. She had told him she was going to visit her mother and that she would only be gone for four days. He had expected her yesterday.

He heard the front door open and close, and when he looked up, he saw Lee coming into the dining room.

"Uncle Hector, we've got the Gatling gun mounted in the turret now, and we're ready to test it."

"Lee, how many times have I told you not to call me Uncle?"

"I know. You said it's because of the men," Lee said. "But I thought when we were alone..."

"It's not just because of the men. It's for you as well. If the men hear you calling me Uncle, then they will not give you the respect you deserve. They will be convinced that you attained your position by way of family connections, rather than through your own initiative."

"Yes, sir," Lee said.

"The fact that it's true, that you hold your position only because of a promise I made to my late wife, makes no difference. The men must think you are one of them."

"Yes, General."

"And another thing," Laroche continued. "There had better never be another example of what happened last week. It is being said all over the county that you hired a couple of Mexicans to take care of a personal problem for you and because of that, one of them is blind in one eye and the other has a cracked rib."

"If they weren't able to handle the job, they shouldn't have taken it," Lee replied.

"Maybe not. But the fact remains you hired someone else to fight your battles. It doesn't look good, not for you, and not for me. See that it doesn't happen again."

"*Señor* General, your pancakes," Maria said, returning with a plate piled high with the steaming cakes.

"Thank you, Maria," Laroche said. He scooped three tablespoons of butter from the butter tub. Then, as the butter melted and cascaded down on every side, he poured on a generous amount of syrup. "Has your sister returned?" he asked Lee.

"No, sir."

"I want you to go to your mother's house and get Anita. She was supposed to be back last night."

161

"I'm sure she'll be along soon," Lee said.

Laroche took a large bite of pancakes, then spoke with his mouth full.

"I intend to see that that is so," he said. "Because you are going to fetch her back here."

"Yes, sir," Lee said, obviously not pleased with the task. At that moment, however, he happened to look through the dining room window and saw Anita arriving, driving a buckboard. "What did I tell you?" he said. "There she is now."

"Good. Will you tell her I would like to see her, please?"

"Yes, sir. What about the test of the Gatling gun?"

"You see to it."

Lee smiled broadly. "Yes, sir!" he said. "I'll be glad to!"

A moment later Anita came into the room. She was wearing a long blue dress and a white straw hat, having changed from the men's clothes she had worn when she was at Pauley. She smiled, brightly.

"Did you miss me while I was gone?" she asked, coming over to kiss Laroche on his cheek.

"I thought you were going to be back yesterday," he said, petulantly. "You said four days."

"I'm sorry. Mother wasn't feeling well so I stayed a bit longer than I intended."

"No harm done," Laroche said, reaching up to take her

hand in his. "As long as you're back."

Anita looked at his soft, fat hand on hers, and she shivered in revulsion.

"You must have some of these pancakes," Laroche said, totally missing the shiver. "They are quite good this morning."

Three straw-dummy targets were set up approximately one hundred yards away from the turret-mounted Gatling gun on top of the express car. Lee climbed up into the seat behind the Gatling gun, placed the one-hundred-cartridge magazine into position, sighted on the targets, then began turning the crank.

The gun roared loudly, filling the inside of the turret with eye-burning gun smoke and red-hot shell casings. He saw dust kicking up all around the straw dummies, and from the dummies themselves. The head of one of the dummies was completely cut off by the stream of bullets.

Lee began yelling in excitement as he twisted the crank, and he continued to do so until the last bullet was expended and there was only the rattle and click of the rotating empty barrels.

When the gun was empty, Lee hopped down, then ran out to examine the targets.

"Son of a bitch!" one of the other men said as he too went over to look at the straw dummies. "I've never seen such a thing. Hell, if we'd 'a had these guns durin' the war, we would'a whipped you Yankee sonsofbitches bigger'n all hell."

Lee looked at him. "Yes, but you didn't have them," he said. "We did."

"Reckon you're right," the unreconstructed Rebel said. "Figured there had to be some reason the damn Yankees won."

Laroche held a celebration down at the depot. The volunteer fire department was there, and so was the municipal band. Free food and beer were being served to all who showed up. The occasion was the official christening of the Laroche Express Car.

Laroche made a short speech, thanking everyone for coming.

"As many of you know, I have bought the bank since I came to this fair community," Laroche said. "And I have invited you here today to see the great care I will give to the money that is entrusted to me. Not only while it is in the bank itself, but also, whenever it becomes necessary to ship specie from one location to the other. Behold, the Laroche Express Car!"

Laroche held his hand out toward the car. As if on signal, the covers over the two firing slits dropped down, and rifle barrels were poked through. At the same time the turret on top, which had been facing away from the crowd, spun around so that the wicked barrels of the Gatling gun were facing the crowd. Those who were close enough could see Lee's face just inside the turret.

The crowd gasped, and several women emitted little screams.

Laroche laughed. "Don't worry, ladies and gentlemen," he said. "This is only a demonstration, designed to show you what any potential train robber would see if he were foolish enough to attempt to stop this train."

Lee began turning the crank and the Gatling gun started rattling in rapid fire, the bullets slamming into a large target pinned to the side of a wagon load of hay.

The women screamed in alarm, and the men shouted in surprise, as large chunks of the target were ripped away by the stream of bullets.

As abruptly as it started, the gunfire stopped, and for a long moment there was nothing but the haunting sound of returning echoes.

Finally the shocked crowd regained their voices, and dozens began shouting as one.

"Hey, General, you goin' to let us inside that thing to have a look around?" one of the voices called from the crowd.

"I'm afraid that wouldn't be prudent," Laroche said. "I'm certain that any potential robber would love to know what the inside of this car looks like. But I don't intend to share that information with them.

"I'll tell you this, however. The express car is equipped with the latest model of vault. It is called an American Standard. The door is four-inch-thick steel, and it is locked by four steel bars, each two inches in diameter. In addition, the tumblers are absolutely silent so that no one can pick the lock."

"What if someone blasted it open?" someone in the crowd called.

"Ladies and gentlemen, you could literally fill this train car with gunpowder, then set it off. The car would be turned into kindling wood, but the safe would be unscratched," Laroche said proudly.

"It sounds pretty secure, all right," one of the townspeople said.

"Yes," Laroche replied. He looked over toward the constable. "Would that our jail was as secure."

Chapter Seventeen

Sheriff Martin knew that the Crocketts had killed Hoffman, and he knew they were after him. He looked at the reward posters he had just authorized.

WANTED

The Quantrill Outlaw Brothers

William and Gideon Crockett

For Breaking a Condemned

Prisoner out of Jail

$500 Reward

DEAD OR ALIVE

Though normally this would not be a dead or alive offence, Martin had convinced Judge Hornung to make it so. By putting out these posters, Martin felt reasonably certain that the brothers would be taken care of long before they could exact their revenge on him.

———

The buckboard creaked and groaned as Laroche stepped out of it and onto the wooden platform that surrounded the depot in San Saba. There were nearly one hundred people gathered around to watch the departure of Laroche's special train.

The engine, which was painted dark green with yellow filigree, rode upon huge red driver wheels. It was trimmed out in highly polished brass, and it glistened brightly in the morning sun.

The express car was also green, with Laroche's name rendered on the side, in yellow script. The express car was followed by Laroche's special car, also green, a luxurious vehicle complete with a bedroom, dining room, and kitchen facilities. That was followed by a red caboose. In addition to the train crew and guards, a telegrapher would be making the trip. The telegrapher, who would ride in the caboose, had an instrument, complete with wire clamps, which would allow him to tap into any telegraph line to send a message.

There were a total of six guards, including in the number Sheriff Martin and Lee Glasscock. Lee would be riding in the turret.

When the buckboard arrived, Felix Martin stepped out of the express car and walked over to greet Laroche.

"General, the steam is up and everything is ready," he said.

"Is the money aboard?"

"Yes, sir, it is," Martin replied.

Laroche looked around. "Where is Miss Sheldon?" he asked. "She should be here. She came into town earlier this morning."

"She's on the train, General," Martin said. He nodded toward the second car. "In your private car."

The dispatcher and the train conductor came out of the depot then. The conductor was carrying a sheaf of papers.

"Is everything arranged?" Martin called to the conductor.

"Yes, sir," the conductor replied, holding up the papers he was carrying. "We have track clearance all the way to Kansas City."

"Then, gentlemen, I suggest we get underway," Laroche said. Puffing from the effort, he walked across the platform, then climbed up into his car. He smiled, when the aroma hit him.

"I wasn't sure if you had time for breakfast this morning," Anita said, greeting him at the door. "So I fried some ham and baked some biscuits."

"You did it yourself?"

"Yes. I know you have servants running all over the house, but I wanted to show you that I could be quite domestic, given the opportunity."

"Well, that's very nice of you, Anita," Laroche replied. "Actually, I did have breakfast before I left, but I wouldn't be adverse to a small snack."

"Good, I would hate to think I went to all this trouble for nothing. Now, how do you want your eggs?"

"Fried, over easy, I suppose. But only three of them. As I said, I have already eaten."

"You have a seat at the dining table, General. I'll have your eggs ready for you by the time the train leaves the station."

Outside, the crowd watched as the engineer opened the throttle. There was a hiss, followed by a sudden puff of steam. Metal creaked and groaned. Then the piston began to slide out of the cylinder, pushing the connecting rod against the driving wheels. The engine started forward, taking up the slack at the drawbars between the cars until, with a clacking jerk, the entire train was in motion.

The engineer blew his whistle, and a team of horses, setting at the crossing just beyond the depot, reared. The train, consisting of a powerful engine and a short string of cars, was able to gather speed quickly, and by the time it was at the end of town, it was moving much faster than anyone had ever seen a train travel.

Katie watched the train until it was out of town, then

went into the depot and wrote out a telegram.

TO BILL JONES STOP SORRY TO HEAR ABOUT JOHN'S CONDITION STOP FIRST MEDICINE LEFT HALF HOUR AGO STOP AM SENDING SECOND SHIPMENT NOW STOP

She tore out the page and handed it to the telegrapher. "Send this to Dallas, please."

"A relative?" the telegrapher asked.

"I beg your pardon?"

"The fellow who is ill. John. Is he a relative?"

"Oh. Yes, he's my cousin."

"Would you care to include a love, Mrs. Lightburn? It would only cost six more cents."

"No, what I have written is fine, thank you."

"Very well. That will be seventy-two cents," the telegrapher said.

Katie gave him the money. Then he sat down at the table and began to send the signal.

"That's funny," he said after he operated the key.

"What?"

"The key isn't as crisp as it should be."

"What does that mean? Is the message getting through?"

"Oh, yes, you don't have to worry about that," the telegrapher said. "It's a little slower, that's all, like more than one receiver is connected." He smiled. "Sometimes

171

they do that in the bigger towns, like Dallas. They'll have an instrument down at the depot, and another one in separate telegraph office."

Thirty miles east of San Saba, five horses were grazing peacefully in a grassy meadow near the track. Tim was pacing nervously up and down the track, while Will, Gid, and Colonel Cook were sitting on a small grassy knoll alongside the track. Actually, only Will and Cook were sitting. Gid was lying down, with his hands folded behind his head.

Frank was sitting cross-legged beneath a telegraph pole, holding a sending and receiving instrument in his lap. Already this morning he had intercepted half a dozen telegrams, but he had discounted them all as being not important.

Suddenly the machine started clacking. Tim looked up from where he was on the track. Will, who was sucking on the root of a grass stem, tossed it away. Gid sat up. Colonel Cook walked over to stand beside Frank.

Frank nodded. "This is it, boys. This is what we've been waiting for," he said. He began writing. After the clacking stopped, he read the message:

TO BILL JONES STOP SORRY TO HEAR ABOUT JOHN'S CONDITION. STOP. FIRST MEDICINE LEFT HALF HOUR AGO STOP AM SENDING SECOND

SHIPMENT NOW STOP

"We've only got half an hour between the pilot engine and the train," Will said. "That doesn't give us much time."

"Where are we going? To the bridge?" Gid asked.

Will nodded. "The bridge," he said.

Katie's father and Uncle Walt Biddle were in the jailhouse, drinking coffee. Although repair had started on the back wall of the jail, it was not yet completed, and therefore there were no prisoners in custody. The few drunk and disorderly cowboys Constable Biddle had rousted during the last week had been released, either on their own recognizance or to the custody of their employer. For anyone with a more serious charge, provisions had been made to transport them to the jail over in Lampasas.

"Did you send the message?" Sam asked his daughter as she came in the front door.

"Yes," Katie said, pouring herself a cup of coffee.

"I hope everything goes all right," Sam said.

"If I know the Crockett brothers, we have nothing to worry about. They are the best when it comes to things like this." Biddle said. "I saw them during the war, when Quantrill spent a winter here in Texas. I recognized them right off... but I didn't say anything because I didn't want to scare them away."

"Then that brings up the next question," Sam said.

"And it's a big one."

"I know what you're going to ask. Can we trust them?" Biddle said.

"Well, can we?"

Biddle rubbed his chin. "I don't know. Right now they don't know anything about our involvement. When they find out...well... we'll just have to wait and see how they take it."

"And if they don't take it well?" Sam asked.

"I asked that same question to Colonel Cook and he said let him worry about it, so that's just what I'm going to do. And I suggest you do the same."

"Well, I'm not worried about them at all," Katie said. "I've never met anyone like Will before. I'd be willing to put my fate entirely in his hands."

"I'm glad you feel that way, my dear, for that is exactly what you have done," Biddle said.

Will, Gid, and Tim were hiding in some bushes, just out of sight from the track. They had a large bucket of grease with them. Frank had left a few minutes earlier, but now he came running back. Only Cook was missing. He had taken the horses ten miles down the track. If everything went as planned, the men would get on the train, take the money, and then be off at about the place where Cook would be waiting. That way they would have fresh horses ready for their getaway.

"The pilot engine is just now coming around the curve," Frank said, panting from the exertion of his run.

"Okay, boys," Will said. "Get ready. As soon as the pilot engine has passed, we have less than thirty minutes to get the rails greased and get up on the trestle."

"How much grease do we have to put down?" Tim asked.

"I'd say at least a hundred yards," Will said. "Otherwise the train won't lose traction long enough to amount to anything."

"Thirty minutes isn't much time to put down one hundred yards," Gid said.

"Yeah," Will agreed. "And we may not even have that much time if the train has caught up any with the pilot engine."

The pilot engine came by then, the engineer leaning out of the right cab window, staring ahead down the track. The engine hurried by with a hiss of steam and the whirring sound of steel rolling upon steel. It pounded out onto the trestle, thundering in its reverberations. Then, as quickly as it had arrived, it was gone.

"All right!" Will shouted. "Let's get that grease down!"

The four men climbed up to the track and began applying a thick layer of grease onto the rails. As they put it down, the grease glistened blackly in the noonday sun.

After only a few minutes, they heard a whistle in the distance.

"Damn, it hasn't been anywhere close to thirty minutes!" Gid said in agitation.

"Yeah, I was afraid they might have closed the gap between them," Will said. He grabbed the bail of the bucket, then slung the remaining grease far out into the bushes. "All right, boys. Up onto the trestle," he ordered.

"Will, how much do you reckon we got done?" Gid asked.

Will looked at the track. "I would say no more than fifty yards."

"You think fifty yards of grease is going to be enough to do the trick?"

"It has to be. Remember, we don't have to actually stop the train. All we have to do is slow it enough to allow us to drop down onto it from the top of the trestle,"

"I'm not all that happy about dropping down onto a moving train," Tim said.

"You'll make it all right," Will said. "All you have to do is think about what will happen to you if you don't. If you miss it, you'll be stuck out here without your horse and without your share of the money."

Tim grinned sheepishly. "I reckon that's enough proddin' all right."

"Son of a bitch!" Gid said, grinning broadly. "We're

176

goin' to do it, aren't we? By damn, we're really goin' to pull this off."

"If we all do our part," Will agreed.

They climbed on top of the trestle.

"Now all of you, lay down." Will ordered. "We can't take any chances on the engineer or fireman seeing us."

Once again the approaching train whistled and this time, when the boys looked up, they could see it coming around the wide, sweeping curve the track made on its approach.

"Get ready!" Will shouted.

The sound changed when the train hit the long grease slick. There was a sudden acceleration of the steam-relief valve. The great driver wheels lost traction, then began spinning. The train jerked and clacked at the sudden change in its propulsion dynamics, then it slowed considerably.

"What's happening to the train?" Laroche asked the conductor. "Why are we slowing down?"

"That happens on occasion, General," the conductor replied, looking out the window. "If a section of rail gets flattened out a little, it sometimes gets very slick and the wheels lose traction. I expect we'll be across it in a moment."

Looking out the window as well, Anita saw that they

were passing onto the trestle. Then she saw something else, something that she didn't want the conductor to see.

"Conductor, would you ask the porter to bring some more coffee, please?"

"Yes, ma'am," the conductor said, turning away from the window.

"And another one of those cakes," Laroche called toward the conductor.

Anita continued to look out the window at the shadow the train cast onto the water, and on the opposite bank of the Lampasas River. The shadow showed four men dropping, one by one from the trestle, onto the top of the train.

Chapter Eighteen

As soon as they hit the top of the train they had to lie on their stomachs to make certain they weren't knocked off by the cross-beam at the far end of the trestle. Will found a supporting rod running the length of the top of the car, and held onto it as he watched the support timbers flash by. By now the train had moved through the greased part of the track, and was beginning to build up speed again as it threw off the grease that had built up on the driver wheels.

Once they were clear of the trestle, Will lifted his head up to look ahead. Almost immediately his eyes began to water from the smoke that was rolling back from the engine. He turned his face away, blinked a few times, coughed, then looked around on the car to make certain everyone else had made it.

They all had, and they were now lying on top of the car,

holding on against the wind and the jerking movement of the train.

Will got their attention, then pointed toward the opening of the turret. He made a waving motion with his hand to indicate that they should move to the side of the car, just above the door, while at the same time warning them to stay away from the turret opening so that they couldn't be seen.

"Gid, have you got the smoke pot?" he shouted above the wind and the roar of the train.

"Yes, I've got it." Gid answered, patting the haversack he was carrying. He pointed toward the turret. "Looks like we got lucky, Will! There's no one on watch!"

"Yeah," Will replied, "they're either very confident or very stupid." Will looked toward Tim and Frank, and saw that they had moved into position, ready for the next step.

The plan was to introduce the smoke pot into the express car by dropping it down the turret. For now, the car was tightly closed, but when the smoke started pouring out, Will knew those inside would be forced to open the big side door. As soon as the door slid open, the raiders would swing down from the top of the car and let themselves in. They would have the benefit of surprise, plus the advantage of fresh air, whereas those inside would be partially blinded and perhaps confused by the smoke.

"All right, Gid, let's do it!" Will said.

Using his body as a shield against the wind that was being generated by the train's velocity of forty-five miles per hour, Gid struck a match, then lit the fuse on the smoke bomb. He held the bomb until the first bit of smoke began to stream out, then dropped it down through the opening in the turret.

Almost immediately, smoke started gushing out of the turret opening.

"Get ready!" Will said to the others. "That door's going to slide open any minute!"

The men waited, lying on the edge of the car, looking over the edge toward the still-closed side door. From the turret behind them, smoke continued to boil.

The door didn't open.

Will and the others looked at each other in confusion.

"What the hell?" Gid asked. "Aren't they breathin' in there?"

"You sure you got that smoke bomb all the way inside?" Tim asked.

"It went all the way," Gid insisted. "I heard it hit the bottom."

"Well, somethin's wrong," Frank insisted. "How could they stay in there with all that smoke?"

By now the bomb was nearly spent, and the smoke coming from the turret was beginning to grow thinner.

"I'm going to look down inside," Will said.

"Will, be careful!" Gid called. Will nodded, then still on his belly, wriggled back up to the top of the car. He got into position behind the turret, then raised his head and peered over the edge, looking down inside.

The inside of the car was so dark and smoke-filled that at first, he couldn't see anything. Then, when he could see, he saw nothing, not anyone, and not any movement. He raised up from the turret with a puzzled expression on his face.

"What is it, Will? What do you see?" Gid called to him.

Will shook his head.

"That's just it," he said. "I don't see a damned thing. You'd think there would be someone moving around down there."

The train whistle blew.

"What do we do, Will?" Gid asked. "We've got to get inside. We're going to be up to where the horses are pretty soon."

Will looked around for a second, then nodded as if just making up his mind.

"We're going to stop the damned train," he said.

"How?"

"The old-fashioned way. By sticking a gun in the engineer's face."

Standing up, Will, Gid, and then Tim and Frank,

started running forward on top of the express car. They jumped from the car down onto the tender, then moved through the piles of wood until they reached the back of the engine.

At that precise moment, the fireman turned to pick up some more wood. When he saw Will and the others, his eyes grew wide with fright. Will cocked his pistol and pointed it at him, and the fireman backed up with his hands in the air.

"What the hell's got into you?" the engineer asked when he observed the fireman's strange behavior. He turned around then, and seeing Will and the others, raised his hands as well.

"Stop the train," Will ordered.

The engineer shook his head. "Can't do that," he said. "I got orders from General Laroche not to stop for any reason."

"Is General Laroche standing here holding a gun on you?" Will asked.

"No, sir," the engineer said, shaking his head.

"Well, I am," Will said in a growl. "Now, stop the damned train, or I'll shoot you where you stand and stop the train myself."

"All right, all right!" the engineer answered urgently. He pulled on the brake handle, and the wheels locked, bathing the inside of the engine cab with a shower of sparks thrown up from the action of steel wheels sliding on steel rails.

The train decelerated so rapidly that Will had to grab something to keep from falling. The fireman, seeing that as his opportunity, picked up a poker and started toward Will. He got no more than a few steps before Gid dropped him with a solidly thrown punch.

Finally, with squeaks, rattles, hisses, and pops, the train came to a complete stop. The engineer moved the relief valve to vent off the excess steam, and the engine hissed and snorted like some living creature.

"What did you do to my fireman?" he asked.

"He'll be all right when he comes around," Gid insisted. "Pulling a damn fool stunt like that, he's lucky he wasn't killed."

"Get down from the engine," Will ordered. He nodded toward the prostrate fireman. "And take him with you."

"What…what are you going to do?"

"Nothing," Will said. "I just want to make certain you don't do anything either. I wouldn't want this train pulling off without us."

Groggily, the fireman started to get up, and the engineer helped him to his feet. Then the two men, under the direction of Will, jumped down to the ground.

Will, Gid, Tim and Frank got off as well, then started walking toward the rear, keeping close to the cars in order to minimize their exposure to anyone who was on the train and who might take a notion to fight.

From the back end of the private car, a man climbed down and began looking around.

"You the porter?" Will asked, suddenly stepping out from between the cars.

The man had not seen Will, and his eyes grew wide in shock when Will spoke. He nodded.

"Yes, sir," he said.

"Who else is in the car with you?"

"General Laroche is in the car. So is Mr. Morris, the conductor. And, Miss Sheldon, she's in there too."

"Anyone else? Any guards?"

The porter shook his head.

"No, sir."

"Anyone in there armed?"

Again, the porter shook his head. "No, sir. All them with guns is in the 'spress car with the money," he said.

Will stepped up behind the porter. "Let's go into the car," he said.

Walking behind the porter, Will climbed the steps into the car. The entry passageway was narrowed by the bathroom and kitchen. After a run of fifteen feet, the passageway opened up into the lounge area, and there Will saw Laroche, now out of his seat, looking through the window, trying to figure out what was going on.

"'Scuse me, General Laroche," the porter said.

"What is it? What did you find out?" Laroche asked gruffly. "Why did that fool engineer stop?"

"Perhaps this here gentleman can tell you," the porter suggested.

"What gentleman?" Laroche asked. He turned then, made curious by the porter's statement. Will pushed the porter to one side and pointed his gun at Laroche.

"Good morning, General Laroche," Will said.

"What are you doing on my train? What do you want?"

"Why, I've come to rob it, of course," Will answered easily. "But I'm going to need your help."

"Help? You're asking me to help you steal?"

"It should be easy enough for you, General, since you stole all the money in the first place," Will said. "Besides, if you don't order your guards to open the door to the express car, I'm going to shoot you."

"You're bluffing."

"I'm afraid he isn't bluffing, General," Anita said, smiling at Will. "Don't you recognize him?"

"Recognize him? No, I don't. Should I?"

"I would think so," Anita said. "Especially as he and his brother, and the men they rode with, caused you a considerable amount of difficulty during the war. Although, I don't think you ever came face to face with him. I'll let him introduce himself."

"Hello, General. I'm Will Crockett. My brother, Gid, is outside."

Laroche put his hand inside his jacket, and Will cocked his pistol, the metallic click making an ominous sound. "General, your hand had better come back out of there slow and empty," he said.

"I...I was just getting a handkerchief," Laroche said nervously. His hand shaking, he held the handkerchief out to validate his claim.

Will nodded, and Laroche began to wipe the sweat from his face.

"What about it, General?" he said. "Do you help us? Or do you die?"

"I'll...I'll help you," Laroche said.

Will made a waving motion with his gun. "Let's go," he said.

Will ordered everyone off the car so he could keep an eye on them. Then they walked forward toward the express car where Gid, Frank, and Tim were still standing close in, out of the line of fire of anyone who might suddenly appear at the gun ports.

"You!" Laroche said, pointing to Tim. "You are in league with men such as these?"

Will was surprised by the apparent recognition, and he looked at Tim suspiciously. "You two know each other?"

Laroche, sensing an advantage, smiled. "Mr. Crockett,

allow me to introduce someone from the other side. This is Tim Westfall. You have no doubt run into him before. He is the man who killed Bloody Bill Anderson."

"You was a Jayhawker?" Frank asked.

Tim nodded, contritely, then looked at Will. "Will, I'm sorry about not bein' straight with you boys," he said. "Wasn't sure you'd want anything to do with me if you knew who I really was."

"No wonder the only ones you said you know'd was dead," Frank said. "Hell, you kilt 'em."

"Of them three that I named, Captain Anderson is the only one I killed," Tim said. "Though, I fought ag'in you boys enough, I reckon I killed my share of your friends… and I reckon you killed your share of mine."

"And now, you are in league with bushwhackers," Laroche said derisively. "You are a traitor, sir."

"No, sir, I'm not a traitor, General," Tim said. "During the war, I was true blue to the Union. But the war is over now, and we're all goin' our own paths. You got your way of gettin' rich…I got mine. And if there was one thing I learned durin' the war, it was that the bushwhackers did what they did better'n anyone I ever saw. Seemed to me like if I was goin' to put my trainin' to use, it might as well be with the best. So, here I am."

"Westfall, did you ever ride with Otto Hoffman?" Gid asked coldly.

Will held up his hand. "No, Tim, don't answer that," he said quickly.

"Will," Gid said, but Will shook his head.

"Let it go, Gid," he said.

"What do you mean, let it go? Hoffman's the one that raided our farm, killed Ma and Pa."

"Hoffman's dead and the war is over," Will said.

"For us, the war's not ever over," Gid insisted.

"I reckon it's not over for Tim either," Will said. "But the way I look at it, the enemy has changed. And now men like Tim and us are on the same side."

Tim nodded. "I'm glad you feel that way," he said. He looked at Gid. "And Gid, I'll answer your question. I wasn't with Hoffman, but I have to confess that I did things just as bad as anything Hoffman ever did."

Gid was silent for a long moment. Then he shrugged. "Hell," he finally said. "So have I. And I reckon Will's right. We're on the same side now."

"Good move, General, trying to get us to fight among ourselves," Will said. "But it didn't work. Now get this door open."

"Hell, we don't need him for that," Frank said. "Why don't we just kill the sonofabitch and blast the door open?"

"No, no!" Laroche said. "Martin! Martin, open the door! They've got me covered! Open the door, they'll shoot if you don't!"

Laroche's shout was met with silence.

"Will, there's somethin' fishy about this," Gid said. "We've not heard a sound since we stopped the train."

Will raised his pistol and pointed it at Laroche. "Try again," he ordered.

"Martin, I'm ordering you to open the door!" Laroche said. He stepped up to the door and banged on it. When he did, it slipped open about half an inch, and he jumped back in quick surprise.

"Will!" Gid said. "The door's not locked!"

"Yes, I see," Will answered.

Pistols at the ready, the men stood by, waiting for the door to be thrown open.

Nothing happened.

"Get ready," Will whispered.

Stepping up to the door he suddenly shoved it open. A few dying wisps of smoke drifted out, but nothing else.

Will stepped up to the open door and looked inside. "Frank, give me a boost up," he said.

Frank made a stirrup with his hands, and Will climbed up into the car. Although most of the smoke had dissipated, enough of it remained to hang in the bars of sunlight that splashed in through the open door. Will saw someone lying face-down on the floor, and he knelt beside him, then rolled him over. There was a bullet hole in his forehead. He dragged him over to the door.

"Who's that?" Gid asked.

"It's Abe Zahn, my accountant," Laroche said. "You didn't have to kill him."

"We didn't kill him," Will answered.

"What do you mean, you didn't kill him? If you didn't, who did?"

"Maybe the same one who did that," Will said, pointing across the car toward a vault. The door of the vault was wide open, and the shelves inside the vault were bare.

"My money! What happened to my money? Martin!" Laroche leaned his head into the car and looked around. "Martin, where are you?"

"If you want my guess, find the money, and you'll find Martin."

"That thieving, double-crossing bastard!" Laroche swore. "The guards are gone too, aren't they? They were all in it together. Martin, the guards, my worthless nephew. All in it together."

Will looked around the car, then, when he glanced up, he saw something that held his gaze for a moment.

"No," he said. "I don't think Glasscock was part of the deal." He pointed to the top of the car.

"What is it?" Anita asked anxiously. She stepped up to the opening of the car, then looked up toward the turret. Lee, who was obviously dead, was slumped forward against the unused Gatling gun. "Oh," she said. "Lee. Poor Lee."

Chapter Nineteen

One hour before Will and the others dropped down from the overhead trestle onto the top of the express car, the train had stopped for water. When it did so, Martin stepped over to the door and pushed it open.

"Sheriff, you shouldn't be opening the door like that," Zahn said.

Martin looked around at the accountant. The small man, who was wearing a green visor, was sitting on a three-legged stool near the vault.

"Why the hell not?" Martin asked.

"General Laroche left strict orders this door is not to be opened until he says so."

"Is that a fact?"

"Zahn is right, Martin," Lee called down from his perch up in the turret.

"I'm just having a look around," Martin explained.

"You don't need to. I can see everything from up here," Lee said. He put his hands on the ring that surrounded the turret and began turning it through the full 360 degrees. "There's no one out there except the fireman, and he's putting water into the tank."

"What about you, Pearson? You see anything?" Martin asked.

Jake Pearson, one of the four guards, looked out through the firing slit in front of him. "I don't see a thing," he answered.

Sweeny, Moulton, and Baxter, the other three guards also reported that all was clear.

From outside the train, they could hear the fireman and engineer calling back and forth to each other.

"Get ready, boys, we're about to get under way again," Lee said. "The fireman just put the water spout back up and has climbed into the cab."

"Good, good," Martin said. He looked at the four guards and nodded, and they returned his nod.

"Zahn," Martin said. "Open the safe."

"I beg your pardon?" Zahn replied.

"I said open the safe."

"I...I don't know if I should do that," Zahn said. "General Laroche was very clear in his directions."

Martin pulled his pistol and pointed it at Abe Zahn. "I'm glad to see that you follow instructions. Now, let me be clear," he said. "Open the damn safe or I'll blow your brains all over the inside of this car."

"Sheriff Martin, what are you doing? Are you robbing the general?"

"Yes," Martin said. "I'm robbing the general."

Zahn looked around in fear, desperate for one of the guards to come to his aid. The expressions in their faces told him, however, that they not only were not going to come to his aid, they were themselves part of the robbery.

Pearson stepped up close to him. "Are you going to open the safe, Zahn?" he asked. "Or do you need persuading."

"Get out of the way, Zahn!" Lee suddenly shouted. There was a gunshot from above, and Pearson went down.

Sweeny returned fire, and Lee grunted in pain, then slumped forward, his gun falling to the floor.

"Damn!" Pearson said in a strained voice. "I didn't know that sonofabitch had a handgun up there with him. I thought he just had that Gatling."

Martin stepped up to Zahn.

"I'm...I'm not going to open the safe for you, Sheriff," Zahn said.

"You don't have to, you little bastard," Martin growled. "I know the combination." He put the gun to Zahn's forehead and pulled the trigger.

Less than a minute later he had the safe open. The money inside was in six cloth bags, and he started passing it out, one bag to each person. When he held a bag out toward Pearson, he stopped and pulled the bag back.

"Give it to me," Pearson said.

"You think you can keep up with it?"

"Yes," Pearson said. "I'm not hurt that bad."

Martin paused for a moment, then he handed the bag to Pearson. "You lose it and I'll kill you."

"I'm not going to lose it."

With all the moneybags passed around, Martin took out his watch and looked at it.

"All right," he said. "We should be to where the horses are. Everybody out, now!"

Martin slid the door open. Pearson came to the edge, paused for a moment, then jumped out. After Pearson the others went out, one after the other, until it was Martin's turn. With one hand, Martin grabbed hold of the firing slit, then moved outside to hang along the side of the car. With the other hand he pulled the door closed so that, when the train went around curves, no one would notice that the door was open. When the door was pulled shut, he pushed himself away from the car, hit on the down-slope side of the track bed, rolled several times, then got up and brushed himself off.

Martin had purposely left the car last because, by his calculations, it put him nearest the horses. It was his way of discouraging any of the others from deciding to strike out on their own with the money they were carrying. The effectiveness of his plan was proved when he found the horses right where he expected them to be. He then had a leisurely wait of some fifteen minutes before the others showed up. None seemed the worse for their leap from the train, though Pearson was obviously suffering from his gunshot wound.

The little group of riders pushed hard across the purple sage. Martin figured that they had put at least ten miles between themselves and the railroad track. And since the train had continued on even after they jumped from the car, that meant that by now the train had to be at least another forty miles away. He smiled at the way things were going. By the time the robbery was discovered in Dallas, they would be so far away that no one would ever catch up to them.

This robbery was the culmination of a year of work on a plan to divest Laroche of his money. Martin had come up with one idea after another, discarding each idea as being unworkable almost as quickly as it had been conceived. His break had come when Laroche told him that he was beginning to be nervous about keeping so much cash on hand. When Martin suggested that he deposit his money in the local bank, Laroche laughed.

"In San Saba? Have you taken a good look at that bank? It has a safe that could be opened by a child, or blown open with a firecracker! I may as well keep my money hidden in a mattress. No, sir. My money is going to Kansas City where they have a real bank."

"Kansas City? How are you going to get it there?" Martin asked.

"By train."

"Train?"

"A very special train," Laroche said.

Laroche then asked Martin if he would take personal charge of recruiting a guard detail that would oversee the transfer of his money to the bank in Kansas City. Smiling broadly because he could see that the way to Laroche's money had finally been opened to him, Martin agreed immediately.

Martin had let neither the clerk, Abe Zahn nor Laroche's nephew, Lee Glasscock, in on the plan. As he thought back on it now, he realized he should have paid more attention to Glasscock, but who would have thought the cowardly little bastard would have the guts to put up a fight. It would've gone off without a hitch if Glasscock hadn't shot Pearson.

Thinking of Pearson, Martin turned in his saddle to

see how Pearson was doing. Pearson was slumped forward in his saddle, one hand holding onto the pommel, the other stretched across his stomach. The hand he held across his belly was red with the blood that had spilled through his fingers. Sweeny was riding alongside solicitously, leading Pearson's horse.

"Martin," Sweeny said. "Martin, we got to stop for a while and give Jake a rest."

"Pearson took his chances, just like the rest of us," Martin replied.

"Hell, look at him, Martin! He can't hardly even sit up no more, let alone ride."

"Martin, we could all use a little rest," Baxter said.

"Yeah," Moulton added. "Hell, what with the train still goin' and all, we must be near fifty miles away by now."

"All right, there's a stream just ahead, under that clump of trees," Martin said. "We'll stop there, give our horses a blow, and fill our canteens."

"Thanks," Sweeny said. "Did you hear that, Jake? We're goin' to stop and rest for a bit."

Pearson nodded weakly.

It took the riders another couple of minutes to reach the clump of trees. Martin held up his hand and they stopped, then dismounted.

"This is a good place to stop," Baxter said. "We've got shade and water."

"Moulton, get up on that hill and take a look around," Martin ordered. "Make sure there's no one following us."

"Who the hell would be followin' us?" Moulton replied.

"Just do what I say," Martin ordered.

"Baxter, help me get Jake down," Sweeny said.

Martin watched as the two men gently pulled Pearson from his horse, then laid him down. Pearson stretched out on the ground with his eyes closed and his breath coming in ragged, shallow gasps.

"How is he?" Martin asked.

"He's hurt real bad," Sweeny said. He pulled Pearson's hand away, and Martin saw that his entire stomach was covered with blood. "He needs a doctor or he's goin' to die."

"And just where do you plan to find a doctor?"

"I don't know. Maybe Lampasas."

"So we go ridin' into Lampasas about the same time they discover the train has been robbed and two men killed and they send a telegraph message back," Martin said. He shook his head. "You're not being very smart."

Moulton came back down the hill then. "Ain't nobody for miles around."

"Didn't think there would be. But it didn't hurt to check," Martin said.

"What about him?" Moulton asked, nodding toward Pearson.

"What about him?"

"What are we goin' to do about him?"

"Nothing," Martin said succinctly.

"Nothing? We can't just let him lie here and do nothing," Sweeny complained.

"Why the hell not?"

"Because, he's one of us. It could be me, or Baxter, or Moulton, or even you lying here."

"That's right," Martin agreed. "And if it was one of us, we'd be in the same boat."

"What if I go into town to get a doctor and bring him out here?" Sweeny asked. "I could be back before tomorrow mornin'."

"Tomorrow morning? Look at him, for God's sake," Martin said. "He's been gut shot. You ever know anyone to live after bein' gut shot? Doctor or no doctor, he'll be dead before tomorrow morning."

"Still, it don't seem right not to do somethin' about it."

Martin smiled. "I'll tell you what I'll do. Whenever he croaks, I'll let the rest of you divide up his share."

"You know, Martin, now that you bring it up, that's somethin' else I been wantin' to talk about," Baxter said.

"What's that?"

"The shares," Baxter said. "The way you're dividin' things up."

"What's wrong with the way I'm dividing things up?"

"It ain't right, is all," Baxter said. "I mean, you givin'

us only fifteen hunnert dollars apiece, while you're takin' all the rest yourself."

"Now you're gettin' an extra five hundred dollars each," Martin said. "And that was the deal I gave you when you agreed to come with me."

"Maybe so, but it ain't right," Baxter said. "We took the same risk you did. Hell, look at Pearson. He got himself shot. The way I look at it, we deserve a lot more'n any fifteen hunnert, or even two thousand dollars. By my thinkin', it ought to be share, an' share alike."

"Is that right?" Martin asked. His voice was thin and cold.

"Yeah, that's right. And the way I look at it, there are three of us. I figure if need be, we can make you see things our way."

Without the slightest change of expression, Martin drew and shot, his bullet raising dust from Baxter's shirt as it penetrated just below the sternum.

"My God!" Moulton shouted in sudden alarm.

Baxter's face reflected more shock than fear, for Martin's sudden action had caught Baxter completely by surprise. He let out a loud whoosh, as if the air had been driven from his body. Then his eyes rolled up into his head and he fell backward, landing heavily. He flopped once, then was still.

Sweeny and Moulton looked on with a sense of

shocked, disbelief. Martin turned toward them with the smoking pistol still in his hand. The expression on his face had not changed in the least, and seeing him like that, so totally impassive even though he had just killed a man, was somehow more frightening than if his face had reflected rage.

"You boys just got another seven hundred and fifty dollars each," Martin said. "Unless you want to argue about it?"

"No, no!" Moulton said, shaking his head and holding his hands out in front of him, as if warding Martin off. "I'm perfectly happy with how you're doin' things."

"I am too," Sweeny said.

"I'm glad we understand each other," Martin said. He put his gun away. "Throw the money sacks on Baxter and Pearson's horses," he said. "We'll make pack animals out of them."

"What about them?" Sweeny asked.

"What about who?"

"Pearson and Baxter."

"Leave 'em."

"Martin, you can't just leave them here like this," Sweeny said. "I mean..."

"You want to stay with them?" Martin asked.

"No!" Sweeny answered quickly. "It's just like I told you, I hate to leave Jake here without tryin' to do somethin' for him. After all, me 'n him's been pards for a long time, now."

Moulton walked over to look down at Pearson. "Yeah, well, you and him ain't partners no more, Sweeny," he said. "Pearson's dead."

Chapter Twenty

Frank McCain was beginning to wonder if he hadn't made a mistake when he left the Crocketts. They did offer to let him stay with them for a while, and they were good men who he was proud to call friends. Jesse and Frank James were good men too, and so were the Youngers. So were all the men he had ridden with during the war.

There were some who talked about the war, and how bad it was, but not Frank McCain. If he could have it his way, the war would still be going on. During the war he had never been hungry, never without a drink, and most importantly, never without friends. Things were quite different now, when he was broke some of the time, hungry most of the time, and lonely all of the time.

Frank was beholding to the Crocketts for busting him out of jail, particularly as he was about to be hanged. But he didn't want to stay with them. They were brothers and sometimes, even though they didn't mean it, he actually felt more alone when he was with them than he did when he was by himself.

Right now, Frank McCain was sitting in the Silver Dollar Saloon in Brady, a small town in West Texas. Brady was several hundred miles from where the aborted train robbery had taken place. Frank liked it out here where he could move about freely, without the danger of running into some zealous lawman. He was nursing a drink and playing a game of "Old Sol." He would have welcomed a game of poker, but he couldn't afford it.

It wasn't supposed to be this way. If the big robbery he had planned with the Crocketts had gone off as it was supposed to, he would be a rich man now. He could even afford to buy some of that railroad land he had seen advertised when he rode into town this afternoon. Why, he would've had enough to buy this very saloon if he wanted to.

His thoughts returned to the saloon. Maybe he couldn't buy it, but he did plan to rob it. He had never seen a saloon that did as much business as this one. It was the middle of the afternoon and it had been full almost all day. At first, he'd thought he might be able to wait around until a slack time, until there was no one here but the bartender and a few of the whores.

But he had been here for most of the afternoon, and

205

there hadn't been a time when the saloon was completely empty. Now he debated whether he should wait until tonight, when everything was closing down.

The problem with waiting was that he had overheard the bartender talking earlier about taking the day's receipts over to the bank to deposit them. That meant if he was going to rob the saloon, he had better do it while the money was still here.

The bat-wing doors swung open and a man came in and stepped up to the bar. Frank looked up with only a casual interest, until he saw who it was.

It was Felix Martin!

"Let me have a whiskey," Martin said. "And leave the bottle."

"Yes, sir," the bartender replied, sliding the bottle across to him. Martin put his money down on the bar and poured himself a drink. Then he turned and looked around the room. When his eyes reached Frank, they stopped.

"Well, now," Martin said. "Look who's here."

"I...I don't want no trouble with you," Frank said.

"If you don't want any trouble, McCain, why are you here?" Martin asked.

"I was just passin' through," Frank answered.

"Too bad. You shoulda kept on going."

Frank stood up. "I seen 'em, you know," he said.

"You seen who?"

"Them two men on the express car. I seen 'em."

Martin laughed, a short, evil laugh. "Did you? Well, you must've tried to rob that train. I figured with bait like that, someone was goin' to try. I wish I could've seen your face when you found out there was nothin' there."

"What happened to the money?"

"What money?" Martin asked. He shook his head. "There never was any money. It was all a ruse—the guards, the express car, all of it. The real money was shipped by stagecoach."

Frank's eyes narrowed. "I don't believe you," he said. "I told you, I seen the two men you left there."

"You calling me a liar, McCain? I don't like being called a liar."

Frank took a deep breath. "I'm callin' you a liar, 'cause that's what you are."

The others in the saloon began, slowly and quietly, to ease out of the way, leaving a clear line of fire between the two men.

Martin shook his head, slowly. "You should've kept going, McCain. Now, I'm going to have to kill you, and killin' someone always puts me off my feed."

"'Could be that I'll kill you," McCain suggested nervously.

"'Could be, but it ain't likely," Martin replied calmly, confidently.

207

Frank reached down to the table to pick up his glass of whiskey. His hand was shaking so badly, that he had to steady it with his other hand. He turned it up to his lips, spilling nearly as much as he drank. Then he set the glass down and stood there with his hand hovering over his pistol.

"I'm going to let you draw first," Martin said.

Frank's eyes narrowed, and his hand started toward his gun. Martin's shoulder jumped and the gun was in his hand, blazing. His bullet caught Frank in the throat and Frank, surprised by the suddenness of it, dropped his gun unfired and clutched at his throat. Blood spilled between his fingers as he let out a gurgling death rattle. He fell against the table, then rolled off, dead, before he reached the floor.

———

It was six weeks later that Will and Gid walked into the Bull's Neck Saloon in Austin, Texas, having been summoned there by a telegraph message from Colonel John Cook.

"Thank you for coming," Cook said when they joined him at the table.

"You said you had some information that might interest us," Will replied.

"Have you heard from Frank McCain?" Cook asked.

"No," Will answered. "Not since he rode off a month or so ago."

"He's dead."

"Damn," Gid said. He sighed. "Ole Frank always was one for gettin' his butt stuck in a crack. The law hang 'im?"

"No. He was killed by Felix Martin."

"Martin," Will snorted. "We should've killed that sonofabitch a long time ago."

"I know where he is, if you're interested," Cook said. "Martin has the money that you missed when you tried to hold up the train," Cook said. "Or quite a bit of it."

"How much of it?"

"He has bought a lot of property, but we estimate that he still has a hundred thousand dollars in cash."

"A hundred thousand?" Will said. He sighed. "That's a lot less than the amount we started out after."

"Yeah, but there are fewer of us to share now," Gid pointed out.

"Are you interested?" Cook asked.

"Yeah, we're interested," Will answered. "Where is he keeping the money...the cash that he has on hand?"

"I understand that he keeps it in a strongbox in his house."

"That's good to know," Will said. "That makes it a little easier to get to than if he was keepin' it in a bank."

"Where is he?" Gid asked.

Cook shook his head. "I'm not going to tell you," he said.

"What the hell do you mean you aren't going to tell us?" Will asked. "You're the one who brought it up."

"I'm going to tell you, but not yet. Not before we come to some agreement."

"Wait a minute," Will said, holding out his hand. "Are you figuring on trading your information for a bigger cut of the money? Because if you are, you can just forget it. We'll find the sonofabitch without your help."

"No, I'm not asking for a larger cut. That's not it."

"Then what is it?"

"First, I need to tell you that I have just come from the governor's office," Cook said.

"The governor's office?" Gid snorted. "That's a laugh. Hell, as far as I know, the people of Texas don't even have a governor. All they got is that sonofabitch the Yankee army appointed."

"Regardless of how James Throckmorton got there, he is the legal governor of the state of Texas," Cook replied. "And, as governor, he has certain powers that should interest you."

"What makes you think anything Throckmorton might say or do would interest us?" Will asked.

"Because he has given me the authority, on behalf of the state of Texas, to offer you a deal," Cook replied. "Texas will give you a reward of ten percent of any and all monies you may recover from Martin and his accomplices."

"Ten percent?"

"Yes. And a full pardon."

"A pardon? A pardon for what?"

"You and your brother are wanted men in Texas."

"What? Kansas, maybe. Maybe even Missouri. But why are we wanted in Texas?"

Cook took out a dodger and put it on the table before Will and Gid.

WANTED

The Quantrill Outlaw Brothers

William and Gideon Crockett

For Breaking a Condemned

Prisoner out of Jail

$500 Reward

DEAD OR ALIVE

"These reward posters have already been circulated," Cook said. "The only way you're going to get them called back is to take the governor up on his offer."

"Is that what this is all about, Cook?" Will asked. "Have you made a deal with the governor to get yourself a pardon? Well, if you have, you weren't talking for us."

"You don't understand," Cook said. "I'm not trying to make a deal *with* Texas, I'm trying to make a deal *for* Texas."

"For Texas? What are you talking about?"

"I'm an officer of the state," Cook said.

"You are an officer of the state?"

"Yes."

Will finished his drink, then held the empty glass and studied Cook's face for a long moment. Finally, he spoke.

"Well, I'll be damned. You've been workin' for them all along, haven't you? I mean, even when we set this deal up, you were working for Texas."

"Yes," Cook answered.

"You were setting us up?"

"In a manner of speaking, yes, I was," Cook admitted.

"Would you mind telling me who else was in on this little scheme of yours?"

"Everyone was in on it. Everyone, that is, but you two. And, of course, Frank McCain."

"Everyone?" Will asked.

Cook nodded. "Anita Sheldon, Tim Westfall, Katie Lightburn, Sam Eubanks, and Walt Biddle. They were all part of the plan," Cook said.

"Why did you get us involved?"

"We decided that the best time to go after the money was when it was being transported by train. And as Tim Westfall pointed out, you two would be our best bet to do that for us."

"And what did you have in mind for us after we pulled it off?" Gid asked.

"We were going to offer you the same deal I just offered you," Cook said.

"Ten percent?" Will rolled the glass in his hands. "There were nine people involved. Just how far did you expect that ten percent to go?"

"You two and Frank McCain are the only ones who would have participated in the reward. The reasons the others had for being involved had very little to do with the money," Cook answered. "For example, Anita Sheldon wanted to bring down the man she holds responsible for killihg her father. For Sam Eubanks and his daughter, it was the fact that the state of Texas was willing to forgive the back taxes on Brush Creek Ranch, thus returning ownership of their ranch to them. And all Walt Biddle wanted out of it was to be reinstated as sheriff of San Saba County.

"What about you and Tim? What was in it for you two?"

Cook shook his head. "Nothing but the satisfaction of doing our job. We're not eligible for anything."

"You said you are an officer of Texas. Just what is your job?"

"I'm Chief of the Governor's Special Deputy Force, and Tim Westfall is one of my deputies. That means the entire ten percent would have been yours and Frank McCain's.

So you see, the ten thousand dollars would have been split three ways. Now, only two ways, as Frank is dead."

"Still, ten thousand dollars split two ways is a hell of a lot less than we were led to believe we were going to get," Gid grumbled.

"I admit that, but I was taking a chance that you would see it my way," Cook said. "And remember, this would be honest money, you wouldn't have to be looking over your shoulders."

"What if we say no?" Will asked.

"If you refuse the deal I'm going to arrest you," Cook admitted.

"Did you think you could just arrest us without a fight?" Gid asked.

"I hope it doesn't go that far," Cook said. He sighed. "But I'm prepared for it, if necessary."

"Are you also prepared to die?" Gid asked. "Because if you try something like that, you'll be the first one to go."

"Yes, I am prepared now, if need be," Cook said.

"What do you mean you're prepared now?" Puzzled by Cook's statement, Will sensed that something wasn't quite right, and he took a quick glance around the saloon. That was when he realized that they were being very closely watched by several men who had been posing as customers at the other tables.

"Deputies?" he asked.

Cook chuckled. "I wondered how long it would take you to notice that you are surrounded. Yes, these are my deputies. I don't think you really want to try anything now. I'm sure you realize that if you put up any kind of fight at all, both of you will die."

"And some of you as well," Gid warned, menacingly.

"That's true. But don't forget, like you, these men are veterans, and many is the time they have gone into battle knowing that they or their friends might die. That didn't stop them then, and it won't stop them now."

"Cook is right. We won't accomplish a thing except a little killing," Will said. He looked at Cook. "It's your call now, Colonel."

"The offer still stands," Cook said, "ten percent of what you recover and a full pardon."

As Will was contemplating the offer, he looked again at the deputies. That was when he saw Tim Westfall sitting quietly, and unobtrusively, at the table nearest the door. Will nodded.

"Hello, Tim."

Tim nodded back. "Will, it's good to see you again," he said.

Will glanced over at his brother. "What do you think, Gid?"

"It's your call, Will," he said. "Whatever you decide, I'll go along with it."

"All right, Colonel, you've got yourself a deal."

"You're making the right decision."

"Did you say the state has already put out wanted posters on us?"

"Yes."

"Then I want the full pardon for my brother and me now, before we leave town," he said.

Cook smiled, then took out two sheets of paper and handed them across the table to Will and Gid. "I thought you might want something like that," he said. "It's already been taken care of."

"And I want five hundred dollars working money," Will added. "Two hundred fifty each."

"Five hundred dollars?" Cook gasped. He shook his head. "I don't know. The governor didn't say anything about authorizing any kind of fee in advance."

Will forced a smile. "You are Chief of the Governor's Special Deputy Force. Use your influence to talk him into it."

Cook sighed, then pushed his chair back with a scrape and stood up.

"All right, it's a deal. You'll get your pardon and your five hundred dollars. Now, where will I bring the money?"

"Why, with all the amenities this place has to offer," Will replied, taking in the saloon with a sweep of his arm. "You can bring it right here. This is where we'll be."

Chapter Twenty-One

The town of Brady was a hundred and twenty miles from Austin, located at what was currently the western terminus of the Texas Western Railroad. Like any boom town, it was suffering from the effects of growing too fast. Saloons, brothels, and gambling halls were being built faster than stores, schools and churches, so that many of the town's newly arrived residents were less than desirable citizens.

Jess Zeller, owner-publisher of the *Brady Defender*, had lamented that fact often in his newspaper, and today he had just penned another story expressing his opinion, in which he wrote:

Have we sold ourselves for thirty pieces of silver? Have we been blinded by the glitter of gold? My friends, if we are truthful we must admit that the answer to these questions is "yes."

The good citizens of this town have watched with dismay as bordellos replaced boardinghouses, saloons pushed away family businesses, and gambling halls supplanted churches. We have suffered an influx of humanity as new arrivals have come, not to build, but to destroy. The very dregs of society have found their way to Brady. Our streets are filled with drunken and debased men and women who have no regard for decency, nor respect for the rights of others.

And what is the cause of this slide toward Gomorrah? Some might say that such growing pains are experienced by any town that is touched by the railroad. But I strongly disagree with that notion. Hundreds, nay, thousands of cities and towns all across the country have watched the railroad arrive and have benefited greatly from it. Are we to believe that the good citizens of Brady are of such poor stock that they cannot handle what others have handled?

No, I do not believe that. It is not the railroad that has brought such distress to our community. It is the nefarious dealings of one man. One man who has burst upon the scene with thousands upon thousands of dollars which he has spread in such a way as to generate vice and corruption, the better to gain total and absolute control, not only of our business and economy, but of our very souls.

He has acquired enough land through distress sales to

start a ranch he calls the "Bar C." The Bar C has become little more than a haven for desperadoes and outlaws. We have all seen them, the ill-mannered bullies who crowd the decent citizens off the sidewalks, and think nothing of making public displays of their drunkenness and boorish behavior.

It is no secret why the Bar C would hire such men, for it seems more than mere coincidence that the herd of cows at the Bar C ranch is experiencing a growth rate commensurate with the degree of loss in all the other herds of the county. And when neighboring ranchers have made a friendly request to peruse Bar C land for cattle that may have "strayed," they are denied that access by the armed intervention of those same outlaws and desperadoes with which the Bar C is peopled.

How did one man come by so much money that he is able to spend it so freely? Those who have earned money honestly, by the sweat of their brow or the fruits of their labor, are much more discriminating in their spending and investments. It has been my experience that only ill-gotten gains are disposed of in such a cavalier fashion as is the case I have brought before you today.

I think it is time that the owner of the Bar C be thoroughly investigated. We should know the source of his wealth, the better able to judge his intentions. And we should unite to pass laws and ordinances that will greatly inhibit his ability to destroy our town.

Zeller lifted the first copy of today's edition from the platen of the Washington Hand Press, and held it up, the fresh ink glistening black on the page. There was something about a newly printed newspaper, something that stirred the blood and made him want to shout out in pride.

The newspaper in Brady was the third Zeller had published. With a burning zeal to be a journalist and with a heavy freight wagon, he had loaded up press, type, imposing tones, ink, and paper to come West. The other two towns had seemed indifferent to a newspaper. Here in Brady, however, he was actually beginning to make a profit.

But now he felt that all he and the other decent citizens of Brady had worked for was being endangered by the actions of a very wealthy, ambitious, and ruthless man who, though only recently arrived, was taking control of the town and of everyone who chose to live there. He had made the decision, therefore, to do what he could to alert the citizens of the town to the danger that had so recently come into their midst.

"They say the pen is mightier than the sword," he said to himself as he looked over his page. "I guess we're about to find out."

Zeller printed another two hundred copies of the paper,

then carried them out with him, leaving them at locations about town where merchants agreed to sell his papers for him. One such place was the Silver Dollar Saloon. There, he left a stack of fifty papers, picked up four left over from the day before, took forty-six cents from a bowl where people left their money to pay for the paper, then walked back out onto the street to continue his rounds.

At about the same time Jess Zeller was making his rounds, Enoch Sweeny and Ike Moulton were riding up to a house at the edge of town which belonged to a man named Clifford Alexander. Sweeny swung down from his horse, while Moulton remained mounted.

The house was small and unpainted, but the front yard was ablaze with summer flowers carefully planted and tended by Mrs. Alexander. On the side of the house a garden of lettuce, tomatoes, beans, corn, squash, and potatoes flourished.

"That's far enough, Sweeny," a man's voice said, and Clifford Alexander stepped through the front door, carrying a long Civil War rifle in his hands. Behind him, peering tentatively out the door was his wife, a handsome woman in her late thirties.

Sweeny stopped when Alexander called to him.

"Mr. Alexander, no need of you actin' like that," he said. "I come out here to make you a business proposition. Mr.

Cline wants to buy your store, and he is willing to pay a fair price for it."

"I know what his offer is," Alexander said. "And I ain't interested in takin' it."

Sweeny sighed, took off his hat, and mopped his sweating forehead.

"It's hot, Mr. Alexander. Too hot to be standin' out here in the sun talkin' about this. Couldn't we discuss it inside?"

"No need. We got nothin' to discuss. Now you and that fella with you just get on out of here. I see you comin' up my walk again, I won't be so friendly."

Sweeny smiled, and tried a joke. "Why, Mr. Alexander, do you call this friendly?"

"I didn't shoot you on sight, mister. That's as friendly as you're goin' to get from me."

Sweeny sighed, then started back toward his horse. He climbed on, then took the reins from Moulton.

"Mr. Alexander, I wish you'd been more cooperative than this. Our partner is very anxious to own your store, and I believe he will get it one way or the other."

"He don't really want my store atall," Alexander said. "The only reason he wants to buy it is so he can close it and charge folks a lot more for goods they'll be forced to buy at his store."

"Business is business, Alexander," Sweeny said.

In Brady two days later, the homes, schools, churches, stores, saloons, brothels and gambling halls were abuzz with the story of two fires in one night. Clifford and Lena Alexander were found inside their house burned to death.

Normally, the story of two fires in one night would be front page news. But because the *Brady Defender* was the other building that had been destroyed that night, there was no newspaper to carry the story. And, like John and Lena Alexander, Jess Zeller had been found dead in the smoking embers of his rooms, which were located over the newspaper office.

Chapter Twenty-Two

When Will and Gid Crockett arrived in Brady, they looked around at a community where false-fronted shanties and substantial two-story buildings competed with canvas tents for space along both sides of the street. The town was noisy with the sound of hammering and sawing, while half a dozen vehicles of commerce creaked up and down the street. So industrious was the town that two recently burned buildings were already being cleared out, their charred remains being loaded onto wagons that were backed up to the now-empty lots.

"You sure this is the right place?" Gid asked, as the two brothers rode by one of the burned-out buildings.

"You saw the sign outside of town, same as I did," Will answered. "It said Brady, and that's where Cook said we'd find Martin."

"I'll give the town this," Gid said. "It sure as hell is a

busy little place."

"Yeah, it is at that," Will said. He pointed to the Silver Dollar Saloon. "What do you say we start our search in here?"

"That's the best idea you've had all day," Gid said. "I really need a drink. My mouth's got enough dust to plant a field of cotton."

Though it was still mid-afternoon, the saloon was already crowded and noisy with the sounds of idle men and painted women having fun. Near the piano three men and a couple of women filled the air with their idea of a song, the lyrics a bit more ribald than the composer had intended.

"Yes, sir, what can I do for you boys?" the bartender asked, sliding down toward them. He was wearing a stained apron and carrying a towel he used to alternately wipe off the bar, then wipe out the glasses.

"What's your whiskey?" Will asked.

"Got some Old Overholt. Cost you two dollars the bottle or ten cents the drink."

"Leave the bottle," Will said, slapping the necessary silver on the counter.

The bartender put the bottle and a couple of glasses on the bar, and Gid began to pour.

"You boys just passin' through?" the bartender asked.

"Could be," Will said. "Or it could be that we might

stay for a while. This looks like a pretty lively town."

The bartender chuckled. "Yes, sir, it's that, all right," he said. "It started growin' when the railroad come through here. Then a month or so ago, a big investor from the East arrived. He bought up several smaller spreads and built the Bar C, a big ranch just outside of town. And he started spreadin' his money aroun' buyin' up old businesses, buildin' new ones. He's caused the town to really boom."

"Who is this man that's throwin' around all that money?" Will asked, lifting his glass.

"A fella by the name of Cline," the bartender replied. "Some says he's a carpetbagger, but if so, I got no complaints." The bartender made a motion with his hand. "As you can see, his bein' here sure has been good for my business."

"I reckon so," Will agreed. "Cline, you say? You sure that's his name?"

"Well sir, all I know is, that's the name he's goin' by. Martin Cline."

"Martin!" Gid said.

"Yeah, I know," Will answered with a nod. He tossed down a drink.

"You know him?" the bartender asked.

"Could be that we know him," Will said. "Is Cline a big man with a puffy nose and blue eyes?"

"That's him, all right," the bartender said. "He's just

bought a ranch and word is he's hirin' hands, if you boys is lookin' for work."

"We might be," Will said. "How do we find him?"

"The place he bought is just west of town," the bartender said. "You can't miss it. It's a two-story white house, with a huge cottonwood tree in the front yard."

"Well, as I live and breathe, if it ain't Will and Gid Crockett!" a voice suddenly said.

Surprised to be recognized here, Will and Gid turned to see who had hailed them. A big, bearded man, with a wide smile on his face was coming toward them with his hand extended. "Never thought I'd run into you two boys way out here," he said. "I thought you was going to stay in Missouri and farm."

"Fred Bell," Will said, recognizing a man who had ridden with them when they were with Quantrill. "How've you been?"

"Been stayin' out of trouble," Bell said. He laughed. "Or stayin' out of town when I couldn't stay out of trouble. Say, did you boys hear about Frank McCain? He got hisself shot down right here in this very saloon." Bell lowered his voice, then looked around. "Ever' one's sayin' it was a fair fight," he said. "But the fella that shot 'im, this here Martin Cline, purt' near owns the town from what I can find out, so what would you expect ever' one to say? Even if ole' Frank had a chance…he never really had a chance."

"What are you doing out here, Fred?" Gid asked.

"Tryin' to get as far away from all those Yankee car-petbaggin' bastards as I can," Bell answered. "I bought a train ticket, but this is as far west as the railroad would take me. So, this mornin' I bought a good horse and now I'm playin' a little cards, tryin' to raise enough of a stake to go on to California. Say, what about you two boys? You want to go to California with me? They say it's mighty fine country out there."

"We may get out there someday," Will said.

"But we got a little business to take care of here first," Gid added.

"Bell!" someone called from a nearby table. "We're about to deal a new hand. You in or not?"

"I'm in," Bell said, starting back toward the table and the other players. He stopped and looked back toward Will and Gid. "Listen, if you boys ever get out California way, look me up."

"We'll do that," Will promised.

At another table one of the players started picking up his money. "Deal me out, boys," he said.

"You sure you don't want to stick around for a few more hands? Your luck might change," one of the other players said.

"Not today, I'm afraid. I'll see you boys later."

228

As he was leaving, someone from the bar came over to take his seat and the game continued, his absence barely noticed by the other players.

The player who abandoned the game was Ike Moulton, and as Moulton left the saloon he looked over his shoulder toward the bar and the two men he had heard identified as Will and Gid Crockett. He was certain Martin would be interested in this bit of information.

"You're sure it was them?" Martin asked as he lit his cigar.

"I was as close to 'em then as I am to that settee over there now," Moulton said. "And I heard 'em talkin' as plain as if they was talkin' to me. A fella called 'em by name. Will and Gid Crockett, he said. And then they started talkin' like they'd know'd each other for a long time."

"Well, I'll give 'em this," Martin said. "They sure don't give up easy."

"Maybe they're just passin' through," Sweeny suggested. The three men were in the parlor of Martin's ranch house, having gone in there to discuss the news Moulton had brought them from town.

"No," Martin answered. "If they're in Brady, they've come for me, the money."

"What are we goin' to do about it?" Sweeny asked.

"Do? I'll tell you what *you* are going to do. You two are going to kill them," Martin said, easily.

"What do you mean, *we* are going to kill them?" Moulton asked. "What about you?"

"They know me," Martin said. "They've never seen either one of you, so it would be much easier for you to do it than it would me. And don't forget, you have as much at stake in this as I do."

"Not quite as much," Sweeny said. "You've got most of it now."

"It's not my fault that I've invested my money wisely, whereas you two have squandered most of yours on gambling, whiskey, and women."

"Which you let us do, since you now own most of the saloons, gambling halls, and whorehouses," Moulton grumbled.

"I'm not your keeper," Martin said.

"And we're not your soldiers anymore. You can't just send us out to kill the way you could during the war."

Martin looked at the two of them for a moment, then sighed. "All right," he said. "Why don't I make it worth your while? I'll give you ten thousand dollars to kill them, five thousand dollars for each of you. But you must kill both of them."

Sweeny and Moulton looked at each other, then nodded.

"Hell," Sweeny said, answering for both of them. "For ten thousand dollars I'd kill my own mother."

When Martin went back inside he was surprised to see Anita Sheldon.

"Well, what do you want?" Martin asked.

"Money," Anita said candidly.

"Money?"

"Yes, money and lots of it. Because of me, you've become a very wealthy man, Felix Martin. And as you have no doubt noticed, I like wealthy men."

"You mean that fat assed bastard."

"Are you talking about General Laroche?" Anita asked.

"Yes. Did you...?"

"I let him try," she said. "But he was old and fat." She smiled. "That's why I've come to you. That's why I helped you."

"You didn't have much to do with it," Martin said. "I took all the risks to get the money away from the old bastard."

"And how would you have done that if I hadn't given you the combination to the vault?"

Martin smiled. "I guess that did help."

"Hell, yes, it helped, and now I expect to collect what you owe me."

"Well, you're not going to get anything—at least not now."

"Don't test me, Martin," Anita said. "I got Laroche and I can get you.

Part of her reason for giving the vault combination to Martin was to get revenge on Laroche, and in that she had been successful, for Laroche had lost everything. He even lost his ranches when the courts heard the lawsuits filed by Sam Eubanks and the other ranchers, and ruled that the confiscation of their land for non-payment of taxes had been improperly handled.

Laroche had left San Saba a broken and discredited man. So complete was his fall from the pinnacle that Anita almost felt sorry for him as he started the long trip back to Kansas.

But now she had come to Brady to claim her share.

"I was on the train when my brother was killed. I can go to the sheriff and testify that I saw you shoot him," Anita said.

"And I'll say you gave me the combination. You can't blackmail me, Anita."

"Maybe that's true, but who will people believe? A man who is gobbling up businesses right and left, or a grieving sister? I think we both know the answer."

"All right. It's true I don't have any money right now because of all the investments I've made," Martin said. "Give me six months and you'll have your share three times over."

Under the circumstances, Anita had no choice. She accepted his offer.

Chapter Twenty-Three

At the supper table in Mo's Restaurant, Gid ordered a second piece of pie. "What about you, Will?" he asked. "Don't you want some pie?"

"I had a piece already," Will said.

"Well, yeah, so did I, but what difference does that make?"

Will laughed. "It means I'm full. I can't hold another bite."

"Big brother, I never knew what a poor appetite you had," Gid said, smiling in anticipation as a second generous slice of apple pie was put before him.

Will stood up.

"Aren't you going to wait around?" Gid asked.

"And watch you eat? No thank you," Will answered. "I think I'll go over to the stable and check on the horses. If we're going to go find Martin, we need to do it tonight, before anyone gets wind of what we're about."

"Good idea. I'll be ready to go soon as I finish this."

As Will stepped off the boardwalk in front of the restaurant, a bullet suddenly fried the air just beside his ear, hit the dirt beside him, then skipped off with a high-pitched whine down the street. The sound of the rifle shot reached him at about the same time, and Will dropped and rolled to his left, his gun already in his hand. That was when he saw the rifleman standing on the porch roof of the general store, just behind the sign that read, Rafferty's Finest Selections. The would-be assailant was operating the lever, chambering in another round, when Will fired. Will's shot flew true, and he saw the rifle drop to the ground as the ambusher grabbed his throat, then pitched forward, turning a half-flip in the air to land flat on his back. A little puff of dust rose from the impact of his falling body.

Another gunman appeared in the street at that same moment, firing at Will. But Will, with the instinct of survival, had rolled to his right after his first shot. As a result, the gunman's bullet crashed harmlessly into the wooden porch in front of the cafe.

From his prone position on the ground, Will fired at the new gunman and hit him in the knee. The gunman let out a howl and went down. He was still firing, however, and Will felt a bullet tear through the crown of his hat.

Inside the restaurant, Gid had just finished his pie when he heard the shooting. He didn't have to ask what was going on. He knew instinctively that his brother was involved, and he stood up and started for the door, checking his own pistol as he did so.

Will threw another shot toward the gunman, but as his attacker was lying in the street now, he made a more difficult target.

"Moulton! Moulton! Are you dead?" the gunman lying in the street shouted.

There was no answer.

Not knowing if there was anyone else after him, Will got up and ran three buildings down the street, bending low and firing as he went. He dived behind the porch of the barbershop, then rose to look back toward his attacker.

His attacker had also managed to get out of the street, and now he fired at Will. The bullet sent splinters of wood into Will's face, and Will put his hand up, then pulled it away, peppered with his own blood.

"Listen to me!" the gunman shouted. "This here fella is a murderer! There's wanted posters out on him! I'll give a thousand dollars to anyone who helps me kill the sonofabitch!"

"You do your own killin', Sweeny!" someone shouted back. "A thousand dollars don't mean shit to a dead man!"

Will stared across the street, trying to find an opening for a shot, but Sweeny, as he now knew the man's name was, had managed to crawl behind a wooden bench.

Suddenly Will smiled. Sweeny had improved his position by getting out of the street and behind a wooden bench, all right, but it was in front of a dressmaker's shop. And what Sweeny didn't realize was that the large mirror in the window of the dressmaker's shop showed his reflection.

From across the street, Will watched in the mirror as Sweeny inched along on his belly to the far end of the bench. Will took slow and deliberate aim at the end of the bench where he knew Sweeny's face would appear.

Slowly, Sweeny peered around the corner of the bench to see where Will was and what was going on. Will cocked his pistol and waited. When enough of Sweeny's head was exposed to give him a target, Will squeezed the trigger. His pistol roared and bucked in his hand. A cloud of smoke billowed up, then floated away. When the cloud cleared, Will saw Sweeny lying face-down in the dirt with a pool of blood spreading out from under his head.

Will heard someone running toward him then, and he swung around ready, if need be, to take on someone else. When he saw that it was Gid, he smiled in relief, then stood up. Gid joined him, and the two brothers, with pistols drawn, moved to the middle of the street, then looked around with experienced eyes, searching the roofs and corners of buildings for any more adversaries. They saw several people looking at them from positions of hiding, but no one seemed threatening.

"You people!" Will called out, putting his gun away and taking out a piece of paper. "These two men were wrong! I am not a wanted man! This paper is signed by the governor of Texas, and it is a full and unconditional pardon. There's no future in anyone trying to take us on. You're either going to wind up dead, like these two...or if you get lucky and kill us...you will have risked your lives for nothing!"

"Even if you was wanted, I ain't lookin' for no bounty from a Yankee governor," someone said. Will recognized the voice as the same one who had refused Sweeny's offer of a thousand dollars to help kill him. "I'm comin' out, mister, and I ain't plannin' on doin' no shootin'."

"Come ahead," Will said.

When the first man came out and nothing happened, another came out, and another still, until soon the street was once again filled. Only this time, they weren't out as much as pedestrians as they were spectators, for the crowd divided into two groups, half gathered around Moulton's body, and the other half around Sweeny's.

The sheriff came toward Will and Gid, holding his hands out in front of him to show that he had no intention of going for his gun.

"I saw the fight," he said. "Those two men attacked you, and you had no choice but to defend yourselves. But, if you don't mind, I'll just have a look at that pardon you're carryin'. If it's real, I'll start sendin' out wires tomorrow to make certain any dodgers as might be out on you are pulled."

"And if it isn't real?" Gid asked.

The sheriff stopped in his tracks and a flicker of fear passed across his face. Gid laughed.

"My brother was teasing you," Will said, holding the pardon out for the sheriff's examination. "As you can see, this is real."

The sheriff looked at it for a moment, then handed it back. "It look's genuine, all right," he said. "I'll do what I can about getting the dodgers pulled."

"Thanks," Will said. "By the way, Sheriff, do you know either of these men? You have any idea why they would try to kill me?"

"I reckon they were after the reward money," the sheriff said. "They probably didn't know about the pardon."

Will shook his head. "No," he said. "That couldn't be it. They weren't after any reward money."

"Why do you think that?"

"Because I heard this one offer a thousand dollars to anyone who would help him kill me," Will said. "And even if the dodgers were still in effect, the reward was only for five hundred dollars. Why would he be willing to pay double that?"

The sheriff shook his head. "You've got me," he said. "But then, I don't really know these fellas all that well. They came into town the same time as Cline did. As a matter of fact, I think they even worked for him. I know they always seemed to have money to spend. Not as much as Martin Cline, but enough to visit the saloons and whorehouses about every night."

"They worked for Martin?" Gid asked.

"Martin Cline, yes, they worked for him," the sheriff said.

Will and Gid looked at each other.

"So much for our surprise, little brother," Will said. "He already knows we're here."

Chapter Twenty-Four

It had just grown dark enough to light the lanterns when a rider galloped into the front yard on a horse that was lathered from its exertion.

"Damn," Martin said, walking over to the window to pull the curtain to one side.

"What is it?" Anita asked.

"I'm not sure. But something sure as hell is up." Martin took his pistol belt off the hall-tree and strapped it on. Then he put on his hat and stepped outside. Several of his ranch hands, drawn by the galloping arrival of the rider, were also drifting toward the front yard to see what was going on.

"Mr. Cline," the rider called.

"Yes," Martin replied from the dark recesses of the front porch. He came out of the shadows to stand on the steps so he could be seen.

"I come to tell you," the rider said. "That is, I thought you might want to know."

"Know what, man?"

"Your two friends? Sweeny and Moulton? They was both killed this evenin'," the rider said.

"Kilt?" one of the ranch hands said. "How?"

"They was killed by a stranger, a fella named Crockett, I think it was."

"Crockett!" Anita gasped from the shadows behind Martin. "Will Crockett? He's here?"

"Go on back inside, Anita," Martin ordered. "This doesn't concern you."

Anita started to speak again, but the snarling anger in Martin's voice frightened her, so she said nothing more.

Martin looked around at the men who had gathered, mostly from curiosity, in the front yard.

"Men," he said. "The ones who killed Sweeny and Moulton are bushwackers! Their names are Will and Gid Crockett, and during the war, while riding with Quantrill, they burned nearly a hundred farmhouses, almost always killing the innocent men and women they found there. I fought against 'em during the war, so now they're after me. I'm goin' to be askin' for your help."

"I don't know, Mr. Cline," one of the men replied. "I'm the first to admit that the war's over, and I ain't holdin' it ag'in you none that you fought for the Yankees. But if there's some sort of a grudge still goin' on between you and these here brothers, I don't know as I've any right to mix in."

Martin knew that the man had fought for the South in the war, seeing duty at Antietam, Gettysburg, and elsewhere.

"Hagen, these boys aren't like you and me. We were honorable soldiers in an honorable army. These boys were little more than outlaws, using the flag of the Confederacy as a means to rob, kill, and burn."

"He might be right, Hagen," one of the other hands said. "If they was with Quantrill, there's no way you could call such men real soldiers."

"Still, whatever's goin' on between these men and Mr. Cline, it ain't our fight," Hagen said.

"I'd be willing to pay one hundred dollars to any man who would make it his fight," Martin offered.

"Do you mean one hundred dollars a man?" one of the cowboys wanted to know.

"That's what I mean. One hundred dollars to each and every one of you," Martin said. "Plus, a bounty of five hundred dollars for each of the Crockett brothers, payable to whoever actually gets one of 'em."

"Five hundred?" Hagen asked, astounded by the figure.

"For each brother," Martin said. "And since there are two of them, that's a thousand dollars."

"Yahoo! Let's go!" one of the men shouted. "Let's go get them bastards!"

At the shout, several of the men hurried out to the stable to saddle their horses.

It took nearly ten minutes for those who were going to get saddled and ready to ride. Finally they were ready to go, and Martin stood on the front porch, lighted now by the flickering torches carried by the riders. "All right, men," he said. "You know who you're after and you know what it's worth if you succeed. Go find them! And when you do, bring 'em back to me." Martin paused to take a deep breath, then added, "Dead!"

Several of the men let out a yell and nearly two dozen horsemen started out at a gallop.

The riders galloped until their blood cooled, their enthusiasm waned, and their horses grew tired. Then Hagen realized they were just running with no sense of direction or purpose. He pulled up, and because he was at the front of the pack, the others came to a halt with him.

"What is it? What's goin' on?" someone asked.

"Yeah, why did we stop?"

"Well hell, fellas," Hagen said. "We can't just go runnin' around out here like chickens with our heads cut off. We got to have some idea of what we're doin' and where we're goin'. Else we're just wastin' time and wearin' out horses."

"Well, what now?" one of the other riders asked. "I mean, I ain't flatterin' myself that I'm the one who'll get the thousand dollars. But I ain't ready to just give up on the hundred we'll all get if somebody else gets 'em."

"We gotta have someone in charge," Hagen said.

"You do it," someone called.

"Yeah, Hagen, you take charge. For a hundred dollars, we'll even listen to you." The others laughed nervously.

"All right, then," Hagen said. "We're going to divide up. About three or four of you go with each group. That way we can spread out and cover more territory."

"What do we do if we find them?" someone asked.

"If you find them and you kill them, then your group can divide up the thousand dollars among you," Hagen said.

"Yeah, yeah, that's for me," someone said. "I'm for killin' the sonsofbitches and takin' the money."

Within a moment there were as many as five small groups, fanning out in all different directions. Now that they had a sense of direction and purpose, their enthusiasm returned.

Will and Gid Crockett saw a little group of men coming after them. They were sitting calmly on top of a large round rock, watching, as four riders approached a narrow draw. The draw was so confined that the riders would not be able to get through without squeezing down into a single file. It was a place that no one with any tactical sense would go into, but these were not men with a sense of tactics. These were cowboys, fired up by the promise of a hundred-dollar reward just for searching, and another thousand for bringing in the Crocketts dead. There wasn't one of them who wouldn't pull the trigger on Will or Gid if they had the opportunity. Because of that, they were men who could be easily lured into a trap.

Will stood up so he could clearly be seen.

"Will!" Gid hissed. "What are you doing?"

"Setting the trap," Will replied easily.

"Look!" one of the approaching riders shouted. "There's one of 'em!"

"They're up there!"

"Come on! Let's get 'em! Let's get the sonsabitches!"

The riders galloped through the draw, bent on capturing or killing the Crockett brothers, or at least the one they had spotted.

A couple of the men in front thought that Will made an easy target, so they pulled their pistols and began shooting up toward him as they rode.

Will could see the flash of the gunshots, then the little puffs of dust as the bullets hit far short. The spent bullets whined as they ricocheted on by him, though none of the missiles came close enough to cause him to duck.

Almost casually, Will pulled two homemade torpedoes

from his saddlebag and lit the fuses. His elevated position allowed him to, quite easily, drop the blasting charges at each end of the draw. The first explosion went off about fifty yards in front of the lead rider. It was a heavy, stomach-shaking thump that filled the draw with smoke and dust, then brought a ton of rocks crashing down to close the draw so the riders couldn't get through.

The second explosion, which was somewhat less powerful, was tossed behind the riders, bringing the rocks crashing down into the draw behind them, and closing the passage. Will chuckled.

"It's going to be a while before those boys are able to dig themselves out of there," he said.

Will and Gid scrambled down from the rock, then wriggled through a fissure that was just large enough to allow them to pass through. They had left their horses on the other side, and now they mounted, leaving the trapped cowboys behind them.

They rode no more than a quarter of a mile before they saw the next group of riders. Attracted by the sounds of the explosions and the gunshots, they were hurrying over to see what it was.

"There they are!" one of the riders shouted when he spotted Will and Gid.

"Get them!" another yelled.

Will and Gid headed into a mesquite thicket. The limbs

slapped painfully against their faces and arms, but on the positive side, the thicket closed behind them, hiding them from view.

"Gid, lead my horse and keep going!" Will shouted. He hopped down and gave the reins to Gid, who continued to ride.

After Gid rode off, Will squatted behind a mesquite bush and waited.

In less than ten seconds, their pursuers came by. Will waited until the first three had passed before he made his move. Then he reached up and grabbed the fourth rider and jerked him off his horse. The man gave a short, startled cry as he was going down, but the cry was cut off when he broke his neck in the fall.

The rider just ahead heard the cry, and he looked around in time to see what was happening.

"Hey! They're back here!" he called. The rider had been riding with his pistol in his hand, so he was able to get off a shot at almost the same moment he yelled.

The man was either a much better shot than Will had anticipated or he was lucky, for the bullet grazed the fleshy part of Will's arm, not close enough to make a hole, but close enough to cut a deep, painful crease. The impact of the bullet, plus the effort of unseating the rider, caused Will to go down and he fell on his right side, thus preventing him from getting to his gun. The shooter had no such constraints, however, and he was able to get off a second shot. This time his bullet hit a mesquite limb right in front of Will's face, and would have hit Will had the limb not been there. Will knew now that the first shot had not been a lucky accident. This man could shoot.

Will rolled hard, not only to be able to get out of the line of fire, but also to be able to reach his gun. As he pulled his gun up in front of him, though, he saw that it was filled with dirt. He couldn't pull the trigger—if he did the thing might explode.

The cowboy, seeing that Will's gun was clogged, smiled in triumph and raised his pistol for a slow, carefully aimed shot. Will braced himself for it, staring helplessly at the big black hole in the end of the barrel.

Suddenly another shot rang out and Will saw the shooter grab his chest, then pitch backward off his horse. At that moment Gid rode up, the gun in his hand still smoking. He turned toward the other two riders, and they, suddenly realizing that the odds were now even, fired once, then turned and galloped away.

Though the shots were just thrown in the direction of Will and Gid, one of them managed to clip the reins to Will's horse, and the animal, suddenly free, bolted away, leaving Gid holding a severed piece of rein in his hand.

"Damn!" Gid said.

"Never mind, I'll take this one," Will shouted, leaping

onto the horse of the man Gid had just shot.

With both brothers mounted, they began tracking Will's horse down, only to discover that one of the other groups had already found it. The cowboys had dismounted, and were giving their own horses a rest. One of the riders was taking a drink from a canteen, another was leaning up against a rock holding their horses, the third was examining Will's horse, and the fourth was standing a short distance away relieving himself.

Will and Gid dismounted and sneaked up closer on foot.

"It's got to be one of their horses," one of the men said. "It sure don't belong to Cline."

"How do you know?"

"It don't have the Bar C brand."

"Hell, what's that mean?" one of the other men asked, laughing. "Half the animals on this ranch don't have the Bar C brand. And them that do, has it burned across another brand."

"You sayin' Mr. Cline rustles?"

"Let's just say he throws a wide loop." The others laughed. "Hell, we all do," he went on. "Else we wouldn't be workin' here. Why do you think he pays us double what any other rancher pays?"

"Lem, what the hell you doin' over there, anyway?" one of the men asked of the one who was relieving himself.

"What's it look like I'm doin'?" Lem answered. "I'm waterin' the lilies."

"Dammit, you been pissin' for five minutes. At this rate you could hire yourself out as a fire engine."

The others laughed.

Lem came back toward the others, buttoning his pants. He nodded toward the horse. "What do you say we back-track this horse and see if we can find which one of them Crocketts it belonged to?"

"Hell, what difference does it make which one it belonged to?"

"'Cause I figure whichever one it is, is most likely dead or wounded now, 'n more than likely, he's wounded."

"Why do you think wounded?"

"'Cause if he was dead, we'd know it by now. Whoever kilt him would be whoopin' and hollerin' to beat bloody hell, claimin' the extra five hundred dollars. And if he wasn't wounded, we wouldn't have his horse."

"All right, so if we find him, what about the other one?"

"I figure they'll be together. One brother ain't goin' to leave the other. This way we got us a chance of gettin' 'em both."

"You want both of us? We're here," Gid said, suddenly stepping out into the clearing.

"Damn! Where'd you come from?" Lem asked, surprised by the sudden appearance.

"I'll ask the questions," Will said. "Where's Martin?" Both he and Gid had the drop on the four men.

"We ain't tellin' you nothin'," Lem growled.

Will squeezed off a shot and a little mist of blood sprayed out from the side of Lem's head. Lem let out a yelp of pain, and interrupted his draw to slap his hand against the source of his wound.

"You son of a bitch!" he shouted in pain and anger. "You shot off my ear!"

"You've got one ear left," Will replied, calmly. "I'll let you keep it if you answer my question. Where's Martin?"

"I don't know!" Lem grumbled.

Will popped off another shot, and the bullet took away the earlobe of his other ear.

"He's back at the house!" Lem moaned in pain. "That's all I know!"

Will lowered his pistol. "All right," he said. "Take your guns out of the holsters and empty the loads onto the ground.

The men did as they were directed.

"You," Will said, pointing to the man nearest his horse. "Bring my horse over."

The man obliged and Will took the reins from him, then looked at the other four horses. "Let go of their reins," he ordered.

Again his instructions were followed.

Will fired a couple of shots into the dirt near the horses. The animals reared up in fright then galloped off, their hooves clattering loudly on the rocky ground.

"Hey! What'd you do that for?" Lem asked. "It's a long walk back."

"It's going to be longer," Will said.

"What do you mean?"

"Take off your boots."

"What? Are you crazy? I ain't givin' you my boots."

"You can walk without boots or crawl without feet," Will said dryly. "And I don't give a damn which it is." He cocked his pistol again and aimed it at the feet of one of the men.

"No, wait! Lem, shut up! This crazy sonofabitch will do what he says!" one of the men shouted in alarm.

"All right, you can have the boots," Lem said. He sat down and began pulling off his boots. The others joined him.

Gid collected the boots, then walked over to the horse Will had borrowed. He tied the boots to the saddle of that horse, slapped him on the rump, and set him running.

"Damnit! Horse, come back here! Come back here, horse!" one of the men shouted at the galloping animal.

Will and Gid mounted their own horses. Then Gid looked at the four, bootless men and laughed.

"You boys walk just real careful now, you hear?" he

teased. "There's not only rocks and cactus needles out there, you might also want to look out for rattlers. I hear tell they like stinkin' feet." He wrinkled his nose. "And believe you me, you boys do have stinkin' feet."

Gid laughed uproariously at his own joke as he and Will rode away, leaving the four cursing cowboys behind them.

Chapter Twenty-Five

When Martin saw Hagen riding into the front yard later that night, he hurried out of the house to meet him.

"Did you get them?" Martin asked. "Did you kill the sonsofbitches?"

"Not yet," Hagen replied, swinging down from his horse.

"Where are the others? Are they still looking for them?"

"I reckon some of them are. Leastwise, the ones that ain't been killed yet," Hagen answered. He started toward the bunkhouse. "That is, the ones who ain't got enough sense to know better," he added.

"What are you talking about, the ones that ain't got enough sense to know better? And what the hell are you doing back here? Why aren't you out looking for them?"

Hagen stopped and looked back toward Martin. "I told you when all this started that it wasn't my fight."

"But I'm paying you to make it your fight," Martin said.

"A hundred dollars, hell, even a thousand dollars ain't enough money to get yourself killed for. They're your problem, not mine. And if you want to find them, my advice is just to hang around here. They seem pretty determined to get to you. More'n likely they're going to show up right here. And when they do, I don't want to be nowhere around."

"You son of a bitch! You work for me! You can't just walk away like this!" Martin shouted angrily.

Hagen turned his back to Martin, and started toward the bunkhouse. "Oh no? Watch me walk away," he called back over his shoulder.

"You cowardly bastard!" Martin shouted. He pulled his pistol and shot Hagen, hitting him in the back of the head. Hagen went down.

"My God!" Anita gasped. She had been watching the entire scene from just inside the front door. "You just killed your own foreman!"

"The sonofabitch was a coward," Martin growled. He punched the expended cartridge out of his pistol and replaced it with a new load. "Get back inside, and stay out of sight," he ordered.

As it developed, Will and Gid had enjoyed a front row seat to the shooting from their position on a hill about fifty yards from the house. Their inclination was to go up to the house and settle it now, but they had already encountered so many of Martin's men that they didn't know whether there were more back here waiting for them. The brothers' caution was well served when they saw four men running from the bunkhouse, drawn to the scene by the gunfire.

"Son of a bitch!" one of them shouted, looking at the man on the ground. "This here is Hagen! Hagen's been kilt!"

"What happened to Hagen?" one of the men asked.

"I killed him," Martin said calmly.

"You kilt him? Why?"

"Because the son of a bitch needed killin'," Martin said as if that were explanation enough. "Now, you men get rifles and take cover. When the Crocketts come riding in here they'll be easy targets, and the offer I made to the ones who are out looking for them, goes for you too. I'll pay one thousand dollars to see both Crocketts dead."

It was no more than half an hour later when Will and Gid got an unexpected break. Some of the cowboys who had been out on the range searching for the two brothers were now coming back to the ranch. They were tired, hungry, and frustrated over not yet having won any money, and they rode boldly and noisily right up to the ranch. Unfortunately for them, they made no effort to identify themselves.

Those who had remained behind were so nervous that they were jumping at every shadow. They had completely forgotten about the ones who were out on the range, and were totally surprised to see a large body of men ride up on them. It was too dark to see, and they had been made too edgy by the circumstances to exercise the proper caution. One of them put into words what all of them thought.

"Oh, shit! Look at that! The Crocketts have rounded up an entire army!"

A rifle shot rang out from one of the ones back at the ranch, and it was returned by the approaching horsemen, who thought they were being fired at by the Crockett brothers. Their return shot was answered by another, and another still, until soon the entire valley rang with the crash and clatter of rifle and pistol fire. Gun flashes lit up the night, and bullets whistled, whined, and thunked into horseflesh, or buried themselves deep into the chests of some of the hapless cowboys.

"Gid!" Will shouted. "Now's our chance! Let's go!"

As the guns banged and crashed around them, the two brothers sneaked out of their hiding position. They mounted, then rode north for a couple of hundred yards in order to get out of the line of fire. Will had no intention of getting either one of them shot by accident.

Then, during the confusion of the firefight, Will and Gid made plans as to how they would get into the house.

"Look there, maybe we can use that," Gid said, pointing. "That gully winds around all the way up to the barn."

"Yes, but even if we get to the barn, we'll still have fifty yards of open territory to reach the house," Will said.

"What if just I go?" Gid suggested. "I'll burn the barn."

"Burn it?"

"Yes. Once it catches fire, it will create a big enough distraction to let you get into the house without being noticed."

Will smiled. "Little brother, that is a brilliant idea. All right, do it. But be careful."

Gid nodded, then took a deep breath and started running up the gully, keeping his head low. Will watched him until Gid disappeared in the dark.

Shortly after Gid disappeared, the ranch hands discovered they had been carrying on a gunfight with themselves. After much calling and shouting, the shooting finally stopped.

"You dumb bastards! You were shooting at us!" someone called.

"Well you come ridin' in here without a word. What the hell were we to think?"

"Do you think the Crocketts would've come ridin'

in like that? You've done killed Amos and Ernest. And Percy's lyin' back there somewhere gut shot!"

"Yeah, well, you kilt Buster."

"Too bad we didn't kill all of you, you dumb bastards!"

"Look at the barn! The barn's on fire!" someone called.

Will looked toward the barn and smiled. Gid had made it, and now flames were climbing up one corner, licking against the dry shake-shingle roof.

"What the hell! How'd that get started?"

Will made his move then. Running low and crouched over, he darted through the darkness, unseen, to the side of the house. He moved through a grape arbor to the back of the house, then slipped inside through the back door.

"Get some buckets! Get some water on that!"

Inside the house, Will was able to use the ambient light of the burning barn to pick his way through the downstairs. When he reached the parlor he got the shock of his life. He saw Anita, looking through the window toward the burning barn.

"Anita!" he gasped in surprise. "What the hell! What are you doing here?"

"Will!" Anita said, turning toward him. Her face registered shame and fear at having been discovered by him.

"She is with me," Martin said from behind Will. When he turned, he saw the big man holding a gun and smiling evilly at him. "Drop your gun, please."

Will held his pistol for a moment longer, then dropped it and looked back at Anita. "Are you his prisoner?" he asked, though even as he was asking the question he knew that she wasn't.

Martin laughed. "My prisoner? Tell him, my dear. Are you my prisoner?"

Anita stared at the floor.

"Still following the money, I see, Anita," Will said.

"Will, you don't understand," Anita said, her voice racked with guilt.

"You're right, I don't understand," Will said. "Martin, I understand, but not you."

"Actually, I'm using Martin as a first name out here. I prefer to be called Cline." He laughed. "However, there really is no need for you to remember that, since you won't be alive long enough to use it."

Martin made a motion toward the door with his pistol. "Now, step outside," he ordered. "Step outside and call to your brother. He's the one who set fire to the barn, isn't he? A clever ruse that, burning the barn to give you the chance to sneak into the house. Tell him to give himself up."

"My brother will never give himself up."

"Not even to save your life?"

"Hell, no, Martin. Do you really think he doesn't know you're going to kill me anyway? No. He will do exactly what I would do. He'll stay out there in the dark and watch you kill me. Then he'll kill you. If he can't kill you tonight, he'll kill you tomorrow, or the day after that, or the day after that. But I promise you, he *will* kill you."

"Get out there," Martin ordered, pushing him from behind.

With Martin shoving him along, Will stepped through the front door and out onto the porch of the house. By now the porch was well illuminated by the fire from the burning barn, but none of Martin's riders saw them come out, since they were now involved in a futile effort to put out the burning barn.

"Call to your brother," Martin hissed. "Tell him to show himself."

"If you're going to shoot me, you sonofabitch, do it and get it over with," Will growled. "I'm not going to call my brother for you."

"Very well, then you shall have your wish. I'll shoot you now."

From behind him, Will heard the double metallic click of Martin's pistol being cocked, and he waited for the bullet to come crashing into the back of his head.

"No!" Anita suddenly screamed, her scream coming on top of the sound of a gunshot. Will whirled around at the same moment, and saw that Anita had jumped between Martin and him just as the gun had gone off. Now she was staggering away from Martin, her face racked with pain, her chest covered with blood.

"You stupid whore!" Martin roared. He pointed his gun at her, and was about to shoot her a second time. That gave Will the opening he needed, and he closed the distance between himself and Martin in an instant. He grabbed Martin's arm, forcing the gun up just as he fired a second time. This time the bullet went harmlessly into the roof of the porch.

Martin was so surprised by the sudden move that Will was able to snatch the gun from him. But since he was unable to bring the pistol around into firing position, Will did the next best thing. He brought it crashing down on Martin's head, dropping him to the porch deck like a sack of flour.

"Hey, it's Crockett! There he is, up on the porch!" one of the few remaining cowboys shouted, and they started across the yard from the burning barn. Suddenly from behind them, another gun roared, and Gid jumped out from behind a wagon.

"Hold it right there, boys!" he shouted. "Drop your guns, all of you."

By now Will had managed to bring the pistol around so that he too had the drop on the four remaining cowboys. Realizing they were covered, front and back, they had no choice but to do as they were told.

"What do we do now?" one of the men asked.

"Well, you can do one of two things," Will replied.

"What's that?"

"You can die for this sonofabitch who can no longer pay you or" —he paused for a moment— "you can figure that too many of you have already died for him, and you can get on your horses and ride away."

"I don't know about the rest of you boys," one of the men said. "But this one ain't too hard for me to figure. I'm gettin' the hell out of here."

"Me too," one of the others said.

Moments later, nothing remained of the four cowboys but the sound of receding hoof beats.

Martin, who had been temporarily knocked out, was now coming to. Groggily, he sat up, rubbing the bump on his head.

"Keep him covered," Will said to Gid as he walked over to examine Anita. She was breathing her last.

"Will," she said. "I'm sorry. I didn't know it would turn out like this. Can you ever find it in your heart to forgive me?"

"There's nothing to forgive," Will said. "You just saved my life."

Anita coughed, and bubbles of blood frothed from her lips. "Hold me, Will. Hold me."

Laying his gun down, Will took Anita in his arms.

"What do you want to do with Sergeant Felix Martin, here?" Gid asked, stepping up onto the porch then.

"You'll do nothing," Martin said. "Except drop your guns."

Looking back toward Martin, Will and Gid saw that Martin had recovered his gun and was pointing at them.

Martin laughed. "This has turned out just right. I'll kill you two myself and save a thousand dollars."

Martin cocked his pistol, but before he could pull the trigger there was a gunshot and, with a surprised look, Martin slapped his hand over a hole in his chest. He looked down to see blood streaming between his fingers.

"You," he said. "You." He fell back onto the porch.

Will turned to see that Anita was holding the pistol he had lay beside her. She smiled, then dropped the gun and collapsed.

"Anita!" Will called, moving quickly to her.

Fifteen minutes later, Will and Gid rode away from the house, a burlap bag full of money hanging from Will's saddle pommel. Behind them, the barn was fully invested in fire, and its bright light cast flickering shadows upon the bodies of the half a dozen men who had been killed there that night. They were bringing Anita with them.

A Look At: Slaughter in Texas
(The Crocketts' Western Saga: Two)

An American western folklore adventure – bringing justice no matter the cost.

Will and Gid Crockett have joined forces with a fiery redhead – and there's more money in the offing than either could imagine. And this robbery will settle an old score to boot.

AVAILABLE AUGUST 2021

About the Author

Robert Vaughan sold his first book when he was 19. That was 57 years and nearly 500 books ago. He wrote the novelization for the mini-series Andersonville. Vaughan wrote, produced, and appeared in the History Channel documentary Vietnam Homecoming.

His books have hit the NYT bestseller list seven times. He has won the Spur Award, the PORGIE Award (Best Paperback Original), the Western Fictioneers Lifetime Achievement Award, received the Readwest President's Award for Excellence in Western Fiction, is a member of the American Writers Hall of Fame and is a Pulitzer Prize nominee.

Vaughan is also a retired army officer, helicopter pilot with three tours in Vietnam. And received the Distinguished Flying Cross, the Purple Heart, The Bronze Star with three oak leaf clusters, the Air Medal for valor with 35 oak leaf clusters, the Army Commendation Medal, the Meritorious Service Medal, and the Vietnamese Cross of Gallantry.